"I've still got my home,"

Lily told herself as she started digging again, a new determination bringing her out of her temporary lapse into self-pity. "So far, anyway."

From close behind her, a deep, masculine voice that held just a twang of a Texas drawl called out into the wind. "And you've still got me, Lily."

Caught by surprise, her heart beating a swift cadence, Lily twisted in the mud, then stood to wipe the knees of her old, faded jeans. "Mason, you almost gave me a heart attack. You sounded so much like—"

"Like Daniel?" Mason Winslow stepped forward to help his sister-in-law up, a bittersweet smile cresting his face as he took in the sight of her.

Books by Lenora Worth

Love Inspired

LENORA WORTH

grew up in a small Georgia town and decided in the fourth grade that she wanted to be a writer. But first she married her high school sweetheart, then moved to Atlanta, Georgia. Taking care of their baby daughter at home while her husband worked at night, Lenora discovered the world of romance novels and knew that's what she wanted to write. And so she began.

A few years later, the family settled in Shreveport, Louisiana, where Lenora continued to write while working as a marketing assistant. After the birth of her second child, a boy, she decided to pursue her dream full-time. In 1993, Lenora's hard work and determination finally paid off with that first sale.

"I never gave up, and I believe my faith in God helped get me through the rough times when I doubted myself," Lenora says. "Each time I start a new book, I say a prayer, asking God to give me the strength and direction to put the words to paper. That's why I'm so thrilled to be a part of Steeple Hill's Love Inspired line, where I can combine my faith in God with my love of romance. It's the best combination."

His Brother's Wife
Lenora Worth

Published by Steeple Hill Books™

STEEPLE HILL BOOKS

Steeple
Hill™

ISBN 0-373-87082-5

HIS BROTHER'S WIFE

Copyright © 1999 by Lenora H. Nazworth

Visit us at www.steeplehill.com

Printed in U.S.A.

If brothers dwell together, and one of them dies and has no son, the widow of the dead man shall not be married to a stranger outside the family; her husband's brother shall go in to her, take her as his wife, and perform the duty of a husband's brother to her.

—*Deuteronomy* 25.5

To ETC-RWA—
Thanks for your unconditional
support and encouragement.

Chapter One

Lily Winslow sank down in the soft loam at her feet and started digging into the rich, black Texas soil. The old, tarnished garden spade lifted the moist earth away, sending it flying out in a gentle, cascading arc around her knees.

She'd plant more bulbs—maybe some hyacinths, or another bed of gladioli to go with that spot of irises she'd planted earlier in the spring. She wanted color, lots of color in her garden—enough to last all summer.

And then—

She stopped, dropping the spade to the ground as she sank back on her knees and lifted her head up to the sky.

"And then what?" she asked, the summer wind lifting off nearby Caddo Lake to soothe her heated brow. "And then what, Lord? Where do I go from here?"

They'd buried her husband a week ago, and now the loneliness was creeping in around her as silently and swiftly as the water lilies that would soon cover most of the narrow glistening lake sprawled out in front of her.

Looking out over her home, Lily wondered for the hundredth time what she was to do with herself now that Daniel was gone. She'd lived in this small Texas town all of her life, had married a man ten years older than herself, and had watched that man suffer with a disease that couldn't be stopped. Now she had nothing left.

Nothing to fight for, nothing to hope for, nothing to pray for. Not even a child to cherish and raise. Daniel was gone, and her life was just like the place she loved, the small town nestled here on this beautiful body of water.

Uncertain.

"Yep, that's me, all right," she said out loud, her words scaring a fat, brown turtle lounging on a nearby log. The turtle, clearly annoyed about being awakened from his midmorning nap, glanced up with lazy eyes, then slid with a soft splash into the inky blackness of the lake waters.

"Uncertain Lily, in Uncertain, Texas." Lily pushed curling strands of dark brown hair back, tucking the wisps underneath the old baseball cap she always wore when she was working in her garden. Across the bayou, a small blue heron lifted out toward the sky, its slow, graceful flight reminding Lily that some things, thankfully, never changed.

"I've still got my home," she told herself as she started digging again, a new determination bringing her out of her temporary lapse into self-pity. "So far anyway."

From close behind her, a deep, masculine voice that held just a twang of a Texas drawl called out into the wind. "And you've still got me, Lily."

Caught by surprise, her heart beating a swift cadence, Lily twisted in the mud, then stood to wipe the knees of her old, faded jeans. "Mason, you almost gave me a heart attack. You sounded so much like—"

"Daniel?" Mason Winslow stepped forward to help his sister-in-law up, a bittersweet smile cresting his face as he took in the sight of her.

Lily belonged outdoors, with the earth. She was a small thing, as gentle and delicate as the yellow lady slippers, or wild orchids as the locals called them, that grew abundantly around Caddo Lake. Her long dark hair shined with a natural light, highlighted from sunshine and gentle breezes. Her skin was like bronzed satin, and when she lifted her dark, almost black eyes to his face, he could see the trace of her ancestors in her. Lily had descended from the Caddo tribe that had once roamed this land.

She was beautiful, not so much physically, as spiritually. Lily had a rare inner beauty that emerged from a quiet strength and gritty determination to do what was right—always. And his older brother, Daniel, had won her hand in marriage while Mason had been out trying to conquer the world.

He'd conquered the world all right, but sometimes he had to wonder if his brother had won the real prize. Now that brother was dead and buried at the too-young age of thirty-nine—just five years older than Mason himself.

Now Mason had come to take care of the woman his brother had left in his charge. And already he'd frightened her. He could see the fear and uncertainty in the dark pools of her eyes.

"I'm sorry," he said, his hand gentle on hers as he guided her out of the freshly turned soil of yet another flower bed. "I didn't mean to startle you."

"It's okay—I'm okay. What are you doing here?" To hide her surprise and discomfort, she glanced over his tailor-made silk suit and shiny black loafers. Avoiding his blue-black eyes—they reminded her too much of Daniel—she instead concentrated on the furrow in his forehead. "I mean, I didn't expect you back so soon after the funeral."

Mason led her to a nearby cedar picnic table, where a tall glass of lemonade sat sweating in the midmorning heat.

"May I?" he said, taking the glass in his hand.

"Of course," Lily replied. She'd only taken a couple of sips of the cool drink herself, but she certainly didn't mind sharing with Mason. After all, she'd known him all of her life. After he'd taken a hefty drink of the freshly squeezed lemonade, she asked again, "Now, what are you doing here?"

Mason put the glass down, then gave her that direct look that probably caused junior executives back at Winslow Industries in Dallas to quake in their boots. "It's about the will, Lily. I got a message from Jim Stratmore yesterday. He says you haven't been returning his calls." His voice softened with his next words. "Look, I understand how uncomfortable and painful this is for you, but we need to get it over with."

"You mean the reading of Daniel's will?"

She'd tried not to think about that. In fact, she'd been surprised Daniel had even left a will. But then, Daniel had been a meticulous man, always organized in both thoughts and deeds. He would never leave her wondering what to do about things. He'd want everything in order, everything in its place. Including his wife.

Looking up at Mason now, Lily had to wonder just what was her place. She'd been Daniel's wife—she'd loved him, nursed him during the worst part of his illness—yet she'd never been really sure of his feelings for her, or where she stood in his life. And she knew the reason why. She knew why her husband had turned cold and uncaring a few years after they'd been married. She knew, and now that particular knowledge was eating away at her—corroding her soul like swamp waters lapping at a boat wreck. Maybe that was why she'd put off having his will read.

Because she knew in her heart that she had nothing left. Nothing to hope for, to pray for, to live for. And she also knew her feelings of gloom had nothing to do with any monetary gain or material possessions. For the first time in her life, Lily couldn't let faith alone sustain her. She'd have to pray hard to get herself through this, but Lord, she was so tired, so very tired.

As if reading her thoughts, Mason touched his hand to her arm. "I'm here, Lily. We'll get through this together."

She looked up, smiled at him. "We always do, don't we, Mason?"

"We always will," he replied. Then he drank the rest of her lemonade, his hand still on her arm.

"With God's help," Lily reminded him, her tone gentle.

Mason wasn't sure he could agree with her there. Since the day he'd left this remote spot on Caddo Lake near the Texas/Louisiana border, he'd learned to rely on only himself. Daniel had been the devout one, the one who'd taken the word of God literally.

The one who'd taken sweet, gentle Lily as his bride.

But, Mason reminded himself now, as he watched the woman beside him, his brother had also taken Lily for granted.

That was something Mason never intended to do.

But he would take care of her. He'd promised his stubborn brother that much, at least. Lily could always count on Mason Winslow. After all, he was her brother-in-law. She was part of his family—the only part left now that his mother and brother were gone, and his wayward father was nowhere to be found. And it didn't matter that she had family right down the road, a big, loving family that would shelter her and protect her, if she'd let them. Lily liked to do things her way, and that meant not burdening anyone she loved.

No, Mason told himself as he sat there looking out over the home he'd left behind so long ago, Lily wouldn't have to worry about anything. He'd see to that.

It was the least he could do. Beginning with getting her to the lawyer's office in Marshall by noon.

"We've got to go, Lily," he said now, giving her a gentle tug. "Jim set the reading for this afternoon. It won't take long, and we need to see where you stand, what you've got left after all the doctor bills and insurance coverage."

"The insurance ran out long ago," she told him, her tone blank. "But the doctor bills haven't. I imagine they'll keep coming long after daisies start growing on my poor husband's grave."

"I'll help you," Mason told her. "I'll help you sort through all of it and decide what your options are."

"Thank you," she said now, resigned and quiet.

"Guess I can't keep putting this off." She shrugged then tugged off her floral cotton gardening gloves. "I'll go in and wash up, get changed."

Mason took the worn gloves—so delicate and dainty with their pink rose pattern—and placed them on the table. "Okay."

He watched as she slowly moved toward the long screened-in porch of the old lake house. She looked small and fragile in her Texas Rangers baseball cap and big cotton shirt. Her gardening clothes. Lily did so love her garden.

He took a deep breath, his nostrils filling with the scent of Lily's fragrant flowers. Dogwoods, their blossoms white and bright like popcorn, took shelter underneath the cypress trees and tall pines. Azalea bushes almost six feet tall, and rich with hot pink blooms, flanked the driveway. A rose, fat and velvet soft, fluttered near the back door of the sprawling cedar-shingled house, while along the porch railings, vines of blue morning glories lay like decorative necklaces. Lilies, some white and tall, others orange and squatty, filled a round bed in the middle of the broad yard. Impatiens, ranging from bright salmon to deep pink in color, played across the expanse of the walkway leading down to the boat dock. And pansies, violets and purples rioting with bright yellows, ran the perimeter of the wooden lattice border surrounding the bottom of the raised house.

Everywhere he looked, Mason was assaulted with a bright array of colorful blossoms.

Lily's garden. Its bright, springtime display contrasted sharply with the darkness of his mood this
morning.

Mason closed his tired, burning eyes to shut out
that brightness. The peacefulness of this place had
never quite escaped him, no matter how far from
home he'd roamed. Even though he knew he'd never
come back here permanently, this place still filled
his heart with longing.

But it was a longing born of neglect, a longing
that echoed through his heart not so much because
he was homesick, but because he'd purposely forgotten what a real home was like. He'd lived here,
in the sad original version of this very house with
his parents and his older brother—until his father
had abandoned Mason and Daniel and their mother,
and taken off to parts unknown.

That's when Mason had learned that a house
could never really be a home. That's when, as an
eleven-year-old boy, he'd decided he'd never call
this place, where they'd struggled and scraped and
barely existed, home again.

Elly Winslow had died here, waiting for her husband, Curtis, to come back. But Curtis had never
returned to Caddo Lake. And while his poor mother
and Daniel had turned to God for their strength, Mason had never forgiven his father, nor God, for that
desertion.

But now this place had gone through a gentle,
exquisite transformation that took Mason's breath

away. Because of Lily. He'd always remember Lily whenever he smelled the pure, clean scent of her garden—especially the beautiful white lilies with their lemony, vanilla-like fragrance, that she'd been named for. She'd turned this rundown lake house into a real home for Daniel and herself.

And now she was here all alone.

"You still have me, Lily," he whispered as the many flowers danced before him like ballerinas moving across a sun-dappled stage. "And I promise, you always will."

Mason didn't make many promises, because he feared that, like his father, he might not be able to keep them. But somehow, for Lily's sake, for his brother's memory, he'd keep this one.

They arrived in nearby Marshall about an hour later. Stopping the luxury sedan in front of Jim Stratmore's picturesque antebellum-style law office, Mason turned to the woman sitting beside him. "You've been awfully quiet. Are you sure you're all right?"

Lily glanced over at him, wondering how he always managed to stay so calm and in control. She supposed being the CEO of your own company could do that to a man—give him that aura of knowing what he was about, of knowing he had power and ability and self-assured confidence.

Being responsible for the livelihoods of hundreds of employees probably forced a man to take charge and stay in control. Mason had to stay on top of things; in spite of his aloof, sometimes arrogant nature, he wasn't the type of man to let anyone down, especially himself. And since college, he'd worked hard to make sure he would always have the kind of security he'd never had as a child. That drive to succeed had moved him from junior executive to CEO in less than ten years, and kept him going now, always pushing for more.

He was completely different from his brother, Daniel.

Daniel had been the quiet one, the one who depended on God to see him through the best and the worst that life had to offer. Daniel had eked out a living running a bait store and tour business on Caddo Lake; he'd been content to live with nature and all her treasures and wisdom. Daniel, neither arrogant nor assuming, had never expected anything of anyone—except maybe his wife.

And, Lily reminded herself now as she sat there in the protective confines of the car's comfortable taupe leather seats, with soothing classical music on the CD player, she'd failed him miserably. How could she explain this feeling of complete hopelessness, of total inadequacy to Mason? He didn't know the meaning of those words. And he'd probably scoff at her if she tried to explain to him how she felt.

So instead she just smiled and sighed. "I guess I'm just tired. I'm not very good with words, Mason.

You know that. I don't want to make a fool of myself in there." *Or with you.*

Mason glanced over her crisp white cotton blouse and sensible khaki skirt. Even in the plain clothes, Lily looked dainty and feminine, and doubtful. "You could never make a fool of yourself, Lily Winslow. And besides, all you have to do is sit there and listen while Jim goes on and on with legalese."

Lily shook her head. "See…there. I hardly know what that word means, let alone trying to understand it."

"I'll explain everything," he assured her, his hand touching on her arm. "Once you get past the technical stuff, the reading of a legal document isn't as intimidating as it sounds. Mostly just stuffy, overblown words."

"Well, I don't deal in stuffy, overblown words," she responded with a stubborn set to her chin. "I like plain English."

He had to grin in spite of the somber occasion. "Okay, I'll demand that Jim speak in plain, simple English. Now can we go in? This noonday sun is beginning to melt my shirt."

"I'm sorry," she said, opening the door to get out. "I'll be okay. This is…it's just hard to face."

Mason came around the car to guide her up the wooden steps. "I know that, honey. You're still in shock, still grieving for Daniel. You've been through a terrible ordeal, what with all those months of watching him get more and more sick, then having to nurse him to the very end.'' He held her back at the double doors. ''You could use a good, long rest, Lily. You know, I have a condo near Corpus Christi, right on the beach. It's yours for the asking.''

She had to smile at that. ''Mason, I have water right in front of me every day on the lake. And all that sand—I'd probably start digging it up to plant more sea grass or something.''

He laughed at that, easing some of the tension. ''Yeah, you certainly would. You'd have the whole of Padre Island relandscaped within a week. On second thought—''

''On second thought, I'm fine right where I am. It'll be hard—the quiet, the empty house—'' She stopped to squeeze her eyes shut. ''But that's the way it is now, and I might as well get used to it.''

Thinking she was going to cry, Mason reached for her. But he should have known Lily wouldn't cry. She was the strongest woman he'd ever known—much stronger than any of his overstressed, overtheatrical female executives back in Dallas. They could all learn a thing or two from Lily's quiet strength.

He watched as she opened her eyes and lifted her head toward the doors. ''Let's go on in.''

''Okay.'' He held one of the thick wooden doors for her, and they entered the air-conditioned hush of the fancy law office.

A pretty blond receptionist greeted them. ''Hello,

Mr. Winslow, Mrs. Winslow. Let me take you into Mr. Stratmore's office. He's expecting you.''

The young lady guided them down a tiled hallway, then into a large corner office that had a perfect view of the famous historic courthouse across the street. After offering them coffee or iced tea, the assistant nodded toward her boss.

"Thanks, Tina," Jim Stratmore said as he came up from behind one of the biggest desks Lily had ever seen. A big man himself, Jim stood over six feet tall and wore a black string tie around his wide neck and shiny black boots on his even wider feet.

"Lily," he said as he took her hand to guide her to a fat, burgundy leather chair, "I am so sorry about Daniel. He was a good man and one of the best fishing guides on Caddo Lake."

"He'd like hearing that," Lily replied. "Daniel did love that lake."

"It's one of the most beautiful spots on the good Lord's green earth," Jim said as he shook Mason's hand. "Sorry about your brother."

"Thank you."

Mason sat across from Lily, in a wing chair just like hers, his gaze touching briefly on her face. Making sure she was comfortable, Lily imagined. She shot him a quick look, then turned her attention back to Jim's imposing presence.

"I guess you two want to get down to business," the silver-haired lawyer replied, his tone solicitous.

Giving Lily a soft smile, he added, "Lily, I'll try to make this as painless as possible."

At her nod, he continued. "Now let me just get through all the legal talk." With that, he read through the official listing of the will, then he stopped, his bright blue eyes moving from Mason's blank face to Lily's curious one. "This next part is what I really wanted you two to hear, since it concerns the both of y'all."

That caught Lily's attention. So far, the lawyer had told her that she was now the sole owner of the lake house and the surrounding land—since Mason had given his share to Daniel long ago—and that any money left in the bank after the bills, of course, would be hers.

Since the bills were extensive, she didn't have any idea how she would manage to keep the house and the land, but she'd worry about that when she had some time to sort through all of this. Right now she didn't like the concerned look on Jim Stratmore's ruddy face.

"Go on, Jim," she said, worry causing her voice to drop.

Jim Stratmore ran his big hand over his face, then leaned back in his chair. "Now, I want both of you to stay calm about this. Keep in mind, Lily, that Daniel loved you and wanted you to be protected after his death."

"I understand," she said, her gaze bouncing off

Mason's puzzled features. "You're scaring me, Jim. What is it?"

"Here goes," the lawyer said, putting his bifocals back on so he could read the rest of the document in front of him. He cleared his throat, then hesitantly began.

"From *Deuteronomy,* Chapter 25, Verse 5. 'If brothers dwell together, and one of them dies and has no son, the widow of the dead man shall not be married to a stranger outside the family; her husband's brother shall go in to her, take her as his wife, and perform the duty of a husband's brother to her.'"

Jim Stratmore stopped reading, then glanced up at the two confused people staring at him.

"What are you saying?" Mason asked, his words so low they could barely be heard above the din of the central air-conditioning.

Mason looked over at Lily. Her face was as white as the heavy damask drapery pulled back from the ceiling-to-floor windows surrounding the room, and her expression bordered on shock. Since she refused to look at him, he could only turn back to the big man behind the desk. "Explain this, Jim, in plain English, if you don't mind."

Stratmore shot them a sympathetic look. "Folks, in plain language, Daniel...uh...Daniel's last request is that the two of you...uh...get married."

Chapter Two

"**Y**ou're not eating."

Mason looked across the table at Lily, his words rising above the din of the few diners in the restaurant they'd found just around the corner from Jim's office.

When she didn't respond, he added, "Lily, at least drink some of your tea. You don't look too hot."

"I don't feel too hot," she echoed, grabbing her iced tea to take a long, nervous gulp. Finally she looked up, right into his eyes.

And took his breath away. She looked so lost, so hurt, so...alone, sitting there in the bright sunshine filtering through the window beside them.

"Maybe I should just take you home," he said, concern evident in his words. "I just thought if I got some food in you—"

"I don't need food," she replied, her patience with this whole absurd situation clearly gone. "I—I just can't believe Daniel would...expect you to..." She couldn't even say the words.

Mason shook his head, then reached across the table to take her hand in his. He could feel the erratic pulse beating against her tiny wrist. "Lily, just forget about it. Look, we both know Daniel wasn't himself toward the end. He didn't know what he was doing. He didn't realize what he was asking."

"He wrote this will long before that, and you know it," she snapped. Seeing the dark flare of anger in his deep blue-black eyes—eyes that reminded her of her beloved lake and the husband she'd just buried—she lowered her voice and tried again. "I'm sorry, Mason. It's just that this is so embarrassing. Imagine you and me, getting married. Why, that's the silliest thing I've ever heard."

"Daniel didn't think it was silly," he reminded her, his ego slightly bruised that she'd find marrying him so incredulous. But, the truth be told, he himself thought the whole idea *was* ludicrous. What had Daniel been thinking?

For starters, Mason lived in Dallas—easily over two hours away—and Lily would never agree to leave the lake. And he could never force her to leave it. She belonged there. But he didn't. So he couldn't see him moving back to a place he never wanted to return to in the first place.

Logistics aside, this could never work anyway. He

and Lily were as different as Dallas and Caddo Lake. He was a businessman, a confirmed bachelor, a workaholic. Lily was a gentle, kind, hardworking woman with high morals and a good life on the lake she loved. Looking at her now, though, for just an instant, he had to wonder what it would be like to have someone such as Lily as his wife.

No, that could never be, no matter how many promises he'd made to his dying brother. He certainly hadn't promised anything like this. Had he?

Sighing, he raked a hand through his hair. "Daniel always did take the word of God seriously."

"Very," she replied, her fingers toying with a fat potato chip. Tossing it down beside her uneaten chicken salad sandwich, she let out her own frustrated breath. "He took things so literally. But this, this goes beyond anything else he's ever done."

"You're right, of course. It's just not possible. I mean, it is silly to expect—"

"Exactly," she said, some of the tension leaving her face. "We can't honor his request. We'll just forget the whole thing."

"Yeah, that's probably for the best."

Lily sat silent for a minute, then said in a voice so low and trembling that Mason had to strain to hear her, "He always wanted a son, you know."

Mason's heart went out to her. For as long as he could remember, Lily and Daniel had talked about having children. But sadly, no children were ever born into the Winslow household. "You tried, Lily.

You both tried to have a child. You can't blame yourself for that not happening.''

"I could have made him happy," she said, tears forming in her eyes. "If I could have given him that one thing—a child—then maybe I wouldn't be so lonely myself. I'd have something of him, to love and cherish. I couldn't give him the one thing he really wanted, Mason. And now it's too late.''

All of Mason's protective instincts surfaced then. He didn't think he could bear seeing her cry. Crying made him uncomfortable. After fidgeting in his chair, he finally reached across the table to squeeze her hand. His voice terse and wavering, he said, "It's not your fault, Lily. Daniel was a very sick man. Sometimes things just aren't meant to be.''

"I guess not," she replied, blinking back tears of regret. "I just wish—"

"Stop blaming yourself," he reminded her again, his tone sharp. "You tried to get him to agree to an adoption, remember?''

"He wanted his own child.''

"He was a stubborn, proud man, and we both loved him dearly, but my brother had to have things his way. And now this…. Did he actually think we'd agree to this?''

"I'm sure he believed we'd honor this request with all our hearts," Lily said, "just the way he always honored any pledges or promises he made.''

Mason smiled then, the action bittersweet. "He was a real character, wasn't he?''

She nodded. "Yes. Which is why I wish I'd had his child. That would have been such a joy."

"Any child of yours would be a joy," Mason said without thinking. "I mean, I'd love it. Hey, I'd be an uncle."

She looked across at him, thinking he was one of the most handsome men she'd ever seen. Both Daniel and Mason Winslow were handsome, though. Two dark-haired brothers, rugged and windblown, not handsome in a pretty, classic sense. But handsome in character, in strength, in life experience. Yet so very different. Daniel had survived on faith and honor, unable and unwilling to ever let anyone down. And Mason—he'd survived on bitterness and distrust, unable and unwilling to make any promises he couldn't keep.

Sniffing back tears, she said, "What about you, Mason? Have you ever wanted children?"

He dropped his hand away from her wrist. "Wow, that's a loaded question."

"No, it's a simple question. You've never talked about it much."

"And I'd rather not start now."

Thinking she'd touched on a nerve, Lily sat there watching the changing expression on his face. She didn't miss the trace of pain shooting over his features. "Then we won't talk about it," she replied. "And we won't talk about this request again, ever."

"But what about the will?"

"What about it? As you said, Daniel was very

sick. I don't know why he felt it so necessary to include this request in his official will, but I do know that I, for one, don't expect you to honor it.''

"But you would? I mean, if I were willing.''

"I didn't say that.'' She looked away, out onto the lazy sidewalk shining in the afternoon heat.

"But you would honor it, right?'' He tugged on her hand. "I know you, Lily. You're a lot like Daniel in that way. You honor your commitments. Whether you feel comfortable with them or not.''

"I won't do anything immoral,'' she shot back, her eyes going wide.

"I wasn't suggesting anything immoral. This is more of a *moral obligation,* after all. Not something we both really want.''

"No, not at all. And all the more reason to just drop it. I won't be obligated to you, Mason, and I don't expect you to be obligated to me. No matter how much Daniel wanted it.''

He took her hand to guide her up away from the small, round table. "Then it's settled. We'll go back to the lake house and go over your bills—see where you stand financially. I can help you sort through that, at least. As for the rest, we'll just put it out of our minds.''

"Okay,'' she said, feeling better now that they'd talked it through.

Yes, she'd just put it out of her mind. That would be the best thing to do. That was the only thing she could do.

* * *

Later, however, her conscience started getting the better of her. Trying to stay busy while Mason sat poring over bills and accounts at the round oak table in her sunny kitchen, Lily ripped at a head of lettuce. She'd invited Mason to stay for supper. Since she had plenty of food from the neighbors and her family, she had thought sharing it would be sensible.

Now she had to wonder if that hadn't been an excuse. She hadn't wanted Mason to leave just yet. She didn't want to be alone.

Silly, she silently told herself as she sliced fresh cucumbers from her father's garden and threw in fat chunks of tomatoes from that same garden. *You've never been one to be scared of the dark.*

No, she wasn't afraid of the night. She loved her nights here on the lake—the sound of wild animals thrashing about in the woods beyond the house, the night birds calling out to each other, the splash of a big fish out near the dock, the sweet scent of magnolias and honeysuckle reaching her through the open windows. Darkness didn't faze her. But this loneliness that had been creeping in—that was another thing.

It had started right after Daniel had become bedridden. She'd talk to him, cooing and encouraging, but he'd never answer. Sometimes he would open his eyes and they'd follow her around the small bedroom down the hall from the master suite, where they'd set up a hospital bed. But he'd never responded or tried to call out to her.

Maybe it had been the accusation, the disappointment in his eyes, that had brought on this melancholy. Maybe the shroud of certain death hanging over that room had made her less sure of herself and her faith in God or mankind.

In her heart she'd prayed for her husband to find some peace, some relief from his terrible suffering. She knew better than to ask God to spare her husband. She could only ask for God's will and for His strength to get both Daniel and herself through this, no matter the outcome. But then she'd become selfish and wish with all her might that Daniel would just get up and be his old self. She'd wish for him to be free of the melanoma that had invaded his body and taken over all his organs, free of the pain, the sickness, the weakness that had reduced him from a big, strapping man to a pile of bedridden bones.

That's when the loneliness would set in. That's when the nights would become so quiet, so dark with grief, that she had to wonder if she'd ever see the light of day again. And with the loneliness had come regret—regret that she hadn't been a better wife to Daniel, regret that she hadn't forced him to go to the doctor sooner, regret that she hadn't been able to give him a child.

Now, as she stood looking out over the lake where the setting sun was just beginning to cast out a golden net of rich gloaming, she once again felt the pull of that loneliness and regret. Now she had only her memories to console her. Now Daniel was finally at peace.

And she had to wonder, would she ever find her own peace of mind again?

Lily closed her eyes for just a moment. *Please, Lord, help me to heal. Help me to find joy again.* She'd let Daniel down in more ways than one. And now she wasn't even going to honor his final wish. Guilt and regret gnawed at her soul.

No, she didn't want to be alone, because then she'd have to come face-to-face with herself.

From his spot on a high-backed chair across the long room, Mason watched Lily as she worked. She moved about her kitchen with grace and sensibility, never wasting a second or a step. She was efficient, tidy, and...she looked downright miserable.

Duty. Lily set such high store in duty. She was probably over there right now pondering their earlier decision to dismiss Daniel's final wish. Lily would feel guilty and ashamed for not following through on Daniel's misguided plans for her. Just as she felt guilty for never giving her husband a child.

Would she ever get over that? Would she be able to function here in the home she'd shared with Daniel, knowing that she had refused him his last, dying wish?

Steady, Mason, he told himself as he glanced over at the woman making war on the poor dinner salad before her. He couldn't go and get all noble now. Not after he'd told both her and himself that this whole idea was impossible. Besides, Lily would see right through any false nobility on his part. She'd always been able to see right through him.

And he'd always admired her from a distance, thinking he could never find a woman such as the one his older brother had been lucky enough to claim. Maybe that was why Mason never kept a relationship going for long. All the socialites in Dallas couldn't hold a candle to Lily Winslow.

It suddenly hit him that he was being handed a delicate, precious gift. It also hit him that maybe, just maybe, his older brother had seen the chemistry between his wife and his brother—an innocent chemistry that spoke of a mutual affection and abiding respect—and had decided they'd be perfect for each other.

Or would they?

Mutual affection aside, Mason still wasn't ready to rush into anything. Nor, he suspected, was Lily. Besides, he surely didn't want her to come to him out of a sense of duty.

No, if Mason decided to follow through on his brother's pointed suggestion, it would be on his own terms and in his own good time.

Lily turned then, her gaze meeting his, her dark eyes wide with wonder. "Mason?"

"Hmm?" He shifted, glanced back at the papers he'd been absently clutching in one hand.

"Are you all right? Is something wrong?"

"No, no," he said as he stood up to stretch. "Just tired." He waved a hand at the pocket calculator and the mound of papers. "This is going to take longer than I thought."

"I'm sorry," she said, rushing to the table. "You know, I can filter through this on my own. You don't have to waste your time doing it."

Mason took her hand in his, his gaze gentle. "Lily, I don't mind. I want to help. And I know you're more than capable, because I've known for a very long time that you took care of things around here."

She became wary. "What makes you think that?"

He shrugged. "Daniel was terrible with numbers, for one thing. And every time I'd come home, he'd brag about how organized and in order everything was. I bet you stayed up many a late night, going behind him, fixing things."

She had to smile. "I did. At first I just did it to help him out. He'd get so mad at himself, and he'd get mad at me for trying to fix things. So I had to learn to be sneaky, Lord forgive me. But you know, Daniel was so proud. And he thought it was the man's responsibility to be the breadwinner."

"And the mathematician?"

"Yes. I didn't want to undermine his authority, or embarrass him. I just didn't want things to fall behind. After he got sick, I just naturally kept on doing what had to be done. I don't think he even cared at that point.''

"But you cared.''

"Yes. I didn't want us to lose this place.'' She looked away then, out the window where crickets chirped in the nearby swamp. "I still don't want to lose this place.'' She waved a hand at the stack of papers on the table. "But I know it's pretty bad.''

Mason nodded. He had to be honest with her. "I haven't even begun to decipher it, but you're right. It doesn't look too promising.'' Still holding her hand, he added, "Of course, you know I'll be glad to buy you out and pay off everything.''

"No!'' The one word tore at her even as she tore away from his touch. "I won't let Daniel down. I promised him—''

"That you'd stay here, toiling away at this place, for his sake?'' Anger clouded Mason's next words. "Will you take over his bait-and-tackle shop and tour duties, too?''

"If I have to. I'm certainly capable of showing people the best fishing spots on this lake.''

He smiled in spite of his anger. "Oh, I don't doubt that. You'd make it on sheer determination alone. But Lily, you're already exhausted from nursing Daniel and trying to keep things up around here.'' He shoved a hand at the table again. "And you're already way behind. Even if you could make a go of the business, it's a fickle and seasonal business at best. You'll be paying off debts for the rest of your life.''

Angry and embarrassed, she pushed the bills aside so she could set the table for their meal. ''Well, what else do you suggest, Mason?''

The words were out of his mouth before he even had time to think about them. ''Well, how about exactly the same thing my brother suggested? Maybe we should get married, Lily. Maybe that is the best solution to all your problems, after all.''

Chapter Three

"Mason, don't even suggest that!" Lily stared across the kitchen table at him as if he'd lost his head. "We've already discussed that and it is not an option."

Mason stalked away from the table, one hand slicing through his clipped hair. "It might be the only option you have."

"No."

He watched as she moved away, busying herself at the oven, taking out the pot roast her mother had cooked. Stubborn woman. He could see her shutting down, closing him out. And he didn't like being shut out.

"Lily, be reasonable."

Lily carefully set the steaming roast on the counter, then dropped her pot holders down beside it with a flourish. "Reasonable? I *am* being reasonable. I won't marry you just because you…you pity me."

Mason threw up his hands. "This isn't about pity. This is about survival. Either you let me buy this place back, or…we get married so I can help you."

"No to both offers."

Wondering why he suddenly wanted to win this fight, Mason slammed toward the counter. "Lily, at least look at me."

She whirled then, her dark hair flowing over her shoulders. "How can you expect me to just up and marry you, Mason? I just buried Daniel! Besides, marriage is a serious commitment, not to be taken lightly. You're standing there, acting as if this is another one of your business arrangements." Pushing a hand at him, she said, "Look at you—so calm, so sure that you've made the right decision. It doesn't matter how I feel, does it?"

"Of course it matters," he replied. "I just think we should consider this, discuss it like two rational people, weigh all the odds."

"There is no discussion. Now let's eat before this roast dries out sitting on the counter."

Confused and frustrated, Mason watched as she loaded up a plate with salad, followed by a big helping of browned roast, potatoes, carrots and gravy.

Not bothering to look at him, she asked, "Do you want a biscuit with this?"

"Yes," he said, his tone subdued for now. She was right, of course. He was grasping at straws. He didn't even want to be married. And he certainly didn't want children; that wouldn't be a problem since Lily obviously couldn't have children.

No children. That realization brought his head up. If he married Lily, he wouldn't have to father any children. Ever.

He'd never told her he didn't want children. He'd never discussed his feelings regarding children with anyone, for that matter, except Robert Webb, his vice president and closest friend back in Dallas. As he'd often told Robert, Mason didn't want to make the same mistake his own father had made.

Curtis Winslow hadn't lived up to his responsibilities. And deep inside, Mason feared he might be just like his father. What if he couldn't live up to fatherhood?

No matter. He didn't intend to ever find out. Knowing he and Lily would never have children together made this arrangement all the more appealing. And made him even more disgusted with himself. How could he do that to Lily? That would be cruel, to marry her for such a purely selfish reason. She'd be crushed.

Might as well forget it altogether anyway, since Lily still had that stubborn set to her pretty mouth.

Taking the plate, he settled down at the table, then waited for her to fill her own plate. "You didn't get very much there," he told her, his eyes scanning the tiny helping she'd dipped.

"I'm not very hungry."

"You have to eat, Lily."

"I'm a grown woman. I'll eat when I'm hungry, thank you very much."

Throwing down his fork, Mason grunted. "Listen, if you won't consider this...this arrangement, then let me buy you out."

"No," she said, her eyes blazing. "That would be like buying something you already own in the first place."

"You're not making any sense."

"You gave Daniel your half. Now you want to pay me for something you gave to us in the first place. That's almost as ridiculous as you deciding we should get married."

"I didn't decide it. Daniel wanted it that way."

"Yes, but we agreed—"

"Well, now I'm *disagreeing*."

Pushing her plate away, Lily stared across the table at him. "That's exactly my point, Mason. Even if in my heart I did decide to honor Daniel's request, which I can't do, you've made it very clear that this isn't what you really want."

"I just told you I've changed my mind on that."

"No, you haven't. You're only doing this out of some sense of duty, to save this place, to help me. I told you—I don't need your pity, and I won't enter into a loveless marriage with a man who clearly enjoys his freedom."

He couldn't argue with that. Was he pressuring her into this simply because Mason Winslow always had to win, at all costs? Or did he secretly *want* this? Was he using her financial situation and a last request from his brother to win the only thing in the world he knew he could never have any other way?

Watching his silent, somber expression, Lily nodded. "See, your very silence speaks volumes about how you really feel."

He shook his head. "You don't have a clue as to how I really feel, Lily."

She got up to dump the contents of her plate in the sink. "I know how you feel, all right. About this place, about marriage and commitment, about life in general. Daniel told me—and I have eyes, Mason. I can see that you much prefer your corporate world to this world. I won't do that to you. And I refuse to do that to myself."

Well, she'd certainly touched all the right buttons. Sliding up, he sent his chair skidding across the planked floor. "You know me so well, huh? You and Daniel had me all figured out, didn't you? Just because I don't go to church every Sunday the way Daniel did, I'm a perfect example of what a sinner is all about, right?"

Lily backed close to the counter, the hurt and fury in his eyes making her wish she could take back her hasty words. "Mason, I'm sorry. I didn't mean—"

"I know exactly what you meant," he said as he came toward her. "I've never considered you a hypocrite, Lily, but now I have to wonder."

"What do you mean?"

He was so close now, she could see the touch of midnight-blue in his eyes. And she could also see the pain and doubt scattered there like breakers on a stormy sea.

"I mean, you spout out things about me—about how I value my freedom, how I can't make a commitment. Then you say things about yourself, about how you won't enter into a loveless marriage—"

"I mean that," she interjected. "I won't."

Unable to stop himself, Mason reached out a hand to touch her face. "You mean, you won't do it ever again, right?"

Shocked, Lily could only stare up at him. But the honesty in his eyes was too much for her. She tried to turn away, but his hand, so gentle, so warm, held her there.

"Mason, please—"

"You tell me that you loved my brother, Lily. You tell me that you were really happy here with him. Make me believe that, and I'll walk away and leave you in peace."

Humiliated, Lily could only stare at the wrinkled white cotton of his rolled-up shirtsleeves. "How dare you..."

"Oh, I dare," he said, his fingers tender on her face. "I dare, because I saw the truth long before either of you did. Even before the worst of it, even before Daniel became so sick he couldn't walk, I saw it. You were miserable here, Lily. He made you miserable, because he didn't really love you, did he?''

"Stop it," she said as she wrenched away from him, her hands searching until she found the cold support of the tiled countertop. "Your brother has suffered enough. He's dead now. Let him rest in peace, please."

But Mason wasn't through. He'd held this inside too long, and now seemed as good a time as any to air his suspicions. "And what about you? Are you at peace now, Lily?"

That he'd hit on her worst fears only magnified them in her mind and made her want to run and hide. "Leave me alone, Mason. If I can just be alone, I'll find my peace."

Coming up behind her, Mason gently coaxed her around. "No, you won't. I can see it in your eyes. You blame yourself for not giving Daniel a child. You blame yourself for his own incapacity to love you the way a man should love a woman. And…you blame yourself for not loving him as strongly as you wanted the world to believe you loved him."

Refusing to give in, she shook her head. "I did love him. You have to know that. I did love him."

"Yes, you did. But it was more out of duty than a genuine love," Mason said, nodding his head. "You gave him everything and you gave up everything to please him. But it wasn't enough, was it, Lily? With my brother, God rest his soul, it was never enough."

Lily looked up then, her misty eyes searching his face. "How did you know?"

"Because I know you. I know what a kind, loving heart you have. And I hated what Daniel did to you."

She shook her head again. "No. Can't you see? It's what I did to him. In the beginning, we were really happy. But...as the years went on, things changed between us. I...I wasn't the wife he expected me to be."

"You were the best wife a man could ask for. And the only thing that changed was my brother's attitude toward you."

"No, Mason. I could have done more. I should have tried harder to make him happy. But after we found out we could never have children together..." Her voice trailed off while her eyes went dark with memories of the pain she and Daniel had inflicted on each other—a silent pain that shouted louder than any condemning words ever could.

Mason looked down at her, his heart opening and shattering at the hurt in her dark, tormented eyes. How many times had he seen that same hurt over the years? How many family gatherings, such as they were, had he witnessed where Daniel would complain about the dinner rolls being too browned or the turkey being too dry, little things that always managed to undermine and destroy Lily's confidence and happiness? How many times had he stood by and watched his brother belittling Lily's efforts to find her own identity, her own place in this world?

Too many, he decided now. And each time he'd try to talk to his brother about it, Daniel would only laugh and tell him to mind his own business, that Lily was *his* wife and that they were just fine. His high-handed superior attitude always shut Mason out, as if to say, "You're not the Christian I am. How can you possibly understand my marriage?"

"How could a man with so much honor not honor the one person who tried to love him?" he asked Lily now. "I know my brother was good, Lily. I know that. I know he believed in the word of God and he lived up to his promises and his commitments. The people around here thought he was the salt of the earth, but..."

He stopped, looked down at her, his heart, so long cold and buried, lifted up on the soaring wings of a newfound hope. "I believe Daniel knew in his heart that he'd been unfair to you. And I believe that's why he suggested we get married. He wanted you to have a better life."

"And you can give me that?" she asked now, tears spilling over her lashes in spite of her clenched jaw.

"I could try."

She looked up at the man holding her now and lost some of her resistance. His anger had turned to tenderness, his frustration had turned to determination. She felt safe and secure here in his arms. She hadn't felt that way in a very long time, and it was mighty tempting to pull him close and enjoy it. But it was also wrong.

Daniel had never been one to cuddle and touch. Mason, as distant and awkward as he'd always seemed in some ways, was much more comfortable holding her than his brother had ever been. Yet it wasn't enough.

"You were right about me, Mason," she said now, her voice low and trembling. "I won't go through that again. I tried so hard, so hard to make Daniel happy. And...in most ways, we were content living here together. We'd laugh and work hard, but...something was always missing. Maybe a child—I don't know what could have made things better."

She looked up at him now, her dark eyes pleading. "But I did love him, and I prayed for God to let me abide in that love, to cherish it. Only...it *wasn't* enough. It was never enough, and that's my fault." Reaching up, she cupped Mason's strong chin in her hand. "I appreciate what you're trying to do, but...I couldn't go through that again, especially not with you. You mean too much to me."

Touched by her honesty, Mason stood there holding her, the scent of her floral perfume mixing with the scent of honeysuckle floating in through the open window. "I could make you happy, Lily."

"And I could wind up making you miserable, the

same way I made Daniel feel," she said. "Let's not ruin a good friendship, okay?"

"Okay," he said, retreating for now. After all, he had some thinking to do himself. On an impulse he pulled her back. "Lily, can I at least do one thing?"

"What's that?" she asked, sniffing back a fresh batch of tears.

"Can I hold you while you cry?"

"Who said I was gonna cry?"

"You need to cry, darling. You need to grieve, not only for Daniel, but for…what never was and what can never be. Maybe it's time you just let it all out."

Lily's gaze caught his, held him there with a fierce pride that made her look like a noble native princess. "Mason, I'm fine—"

Even as she said the words, however, her eyes misted over and her expression hardened against the onslaught of grief. Then she lowered her head and fell into his arms, the sobs racking her body while he held her tight.

As the velvet-soft summer night settled in around them, Mason held her and let her cry, then he whispered in her ear, "You still have me, Lily. Remember that, always."

Over the next few weeks, Lily remembered a lot of things about her brother-in-law. She remembered the way he'd held her that night, letting her rid herself of the long-held grief that had begun months, maybe even years, before Daniel's death. She remembered the way his strong arms had wrapped her in a cocoon of security, making her feel safe and sane for just a few precious minutes. She remembered the crisp scent of his subtle aftershave, the rasp of a day's worth of beard growth as her cheek had touched on his. And she remembered the feelings being so close to Mason had brought out in her, protective, caring feelings that both consoled and confused her, feelings that she wasn't sure she should be having.

Which was why she was sitting here today, on her mother's back porch, staring out at the lake where her father and younger twin brothers were fishing off the dock just as they'd done for as long as Lily could remember. She needed to be with family right now, to console herself, to find some semblance of calm. She needed some motherly advice, too.

Normally she would have been right down there with her father and brothers, trying to catch the famous ten-pound bass they called "Old Man." The fish had eluded them for many years and as her father, Bill Norton, liked to tell folks, the big bass had only gotten fatter off their offerings. The fun was in the trying, though, Bill said.

Musing over that, Lily now wondered if maybe that had been why Mason had offered to marry her. Was the sport in the trying for him? Mason was a very successful businessman, used to winning and winning big. Maybe being turned down flat had presented him a challenge he couldn't refuse. Maybe.

He'd reluctantly left her that night, promising to find a way to help her out. She'd politely told him to mind his own business. Since then, he'd called her every day, just to check in, he told her. To reassure her that he intended to watch over her. This was a new side of Mason that only intrigued Lily even more. He'd always been so formal, so sure of himself, on his visits home. Always polite, always witty and teasing, yet somewhat aloof. Just performing the duty of visiting his only relatives for short periods during the holidays. Just being a good brother.

Now it seemed as if Mason was willing to be more, to do more. Now it seemed as if his determination had somehow changed him. Just as being in his arms had changed her, Lily thought.

However, there had been no mention of Daniel's request in all of those phone calls. They were dancing around the issue, content to just talk and visit, content to try and pretend things were the way they used to be between them.

But things would never be the same now. Not with this request, this demand, hanging over them. Lily wasn't sure how to resolve this, but she knew sooner or later things would have to change, or she'd go crazy worrying over all of it. She didn't want to lose Mason's friendship, or his support. He'd been a rock throughout Daniel's illness and since his brother's death, too.

The screen door opening brought her head up. She smiled as her petite, dark-haired mother proceeded to baby her a bit.

"Here's your iced tea, honey," Cora Norton said. Placing a tray on the small wrought-iron table where Lily sat, she added, "And I brought out some of those oatmeal cookies your father is so fond of. Thought you might want to nibble."

"Thanks, Mom," Lily said, her smile bright for her mother's knowing eyes. "And thanks for inviting me over for supper. You know I can't refuse your lasagna."

"I hope not," Cora said, taking a long sip of her own glass of tea. "You look like you've lost more weight. Have you been taking care of yourself?"

"I'm fine," Lily said, picking up a cookie just to prove to her mother that she had an appetite. "I've been so busy, though. Going through the accounts, taking people out on tours."

"How's that going?"

"It's going." Lily smiled now as she broke off a hunk of moist cookie. "I kind of enjoy it, you know. I always helped out here and there when Daniel was in charge, but now, well...while I could never regale the tourists with swamp tales the way Daniel did, I'm learning things about this lake, things I just took for granted. I've spotted several bald eagles, just this week. And...I never stopped to think about the cypress trees—some are over four hundred years old."

Cora laughed. "Honey, you don't have to tell me all of this."

"I know," Lily replied, giggling. "It's just that it's such a beautiful spot, and I had forgotten all the lore and all the history." Looking out over the glistening silvery water, she added, "How could I have forgotten?"

"Maybe because you had other things to contend with," her mother pointed out.

Lily nodded. "I guess so. Anyway, I'm doing okay. I'm not scheduling as many tours as Daniel handled, but I've managed to make it through each week with at least one daily. That should help some."

"You mean financially."

"Yes, but it's going to take a miracle to pull me out of the red. I've already sold off everything I can sell—the extra johnboats and...Daniel's prized bateau. I sure hated to sell that boat—he built it himself out of the heart of a red cypress—but I just couldn't bring myself to take it out on the lake anymore."

Cora nodded her head. "I remember that bateau. Your father helped him with the carving. Daniel wanted it to be just right." She sat silent for a minute, then said, "You know, if we could help—"

"Mama, we've talked about that. You and Daddy

are already strapped as it is. I won't tap into the twins' college fund or your retirement money."

"Your dear father appreciates that, daughter. But you know we'd do anything for you."

Lily reached across the table for her mother's small hand. "Yes, and I love you for it. But I'm okay for now. And I'm working on alternatives."

Her mother shot her a shrewd look underneath her clipped gray-tinged bangs. "Such as?"

"Such as offering my services as a landscaper, or maybe baking bread to sell at the bait shop." Nodding toward her noisy teenage brothers, she added, "At least I've got help there."

Cora laughed. "Your brothers need to learn responsibility. It was good of you to let them work in the shop."

"Well, the pay won't be much for now, but so far they've managed to keep things going for me. I'll give them a raise as soon as I can."

"Nonsense," Cora said, shaking her head. The looped dolphin-shaped silver earrings dangling from under her fringed bob tingled like chimes. "Pete and Jeremy don't expect much pay. They're just thrilled to have gas money for that old pile of junk they call a car."

Lily grinned at that. Her brothers had just gotten their driver's licenses the year before, and now that they'd saved up enough to buy their own car, the country roads surrounding the lake would never be the same for it.

"Speaking of brothers," Cora began casually, her big brown eyes slanting upward, "what have you heard from Mason?"

Lily hated herself for jumping. "Well, he calls just about every day."

"How thoughtful."

"And he really is trying to help me figure out a way to get out from under these hospital bills."

"That's noble, considering it's been over a month since the funeral."

"Mother?"

"Hmm?"

Lily tilted her head. "Is there something you want to say?"

Cora ran a hand over her floral skirt. "No. But I think you've got something to say, and I think it has something to do with Mason. You said on the phone you needed to talk—so talk."

Amazed at her mother's intuition, Lily asked, "What makes you think it's about Mason?"

Cora ran a hand over her short hair, playing with her ruffled bangs. "Because every time I've mentioned that man recently, you've managed to change the subject. You know how I feel. I think Mason ought to help you with the place. After all, it belonged to his family once."

"Yes, and now it belongs to me." Lily tried yet again to explain. "And as I've told you, Mason has offered to help, but I want to do this on my own."

Cora shrugged, then started plucking dead blossoms off a nearby geranium plant. "Then what's to talk about?"

Lily braced herself, knowing her mother would be shocked by Daniel's request. But she had to talk to someone, and Cora was the most levelheaded, down-to-earth person in the world. She'd help Lily sort through this, the same way she'd helped her through so many other emotional decisions all of her life.

"Mama, there's something I haven't told you," she began, holding her breath to find her nerve. "It's about Daniel's will."

"I'm listening," Cora stated in a calm voice.

"He had one last request."

"What was it, honey?"

"He…he requested that Mason and I get married." Rushing to explain, she added, "He based his request on a law in the Old Testament—"

"His brother's wife," Cora stated, her expression serious as she thought over this bit of news. "Marriage duty of the surviving brother—in part to carry on the family name, in part to keep the wife from having to rely on a stranger."

"That's it." Lily waited, thinking the surprised look on her mother's youthful face would soon turn to disgust or disbelief. But to her amazement, Cora didn't get angry or indignant.

Instead, her tiny little mother grinned broadly and clapped her hands together in glee. "Now that's an idea, isn't it?"

Chapter Four

"**M**other!" Clearly appalled, Lily hopped up to stand at the sturdy white porch railing. Shaking her head, her gaze focused on her father and brothers, she said, "It's a very bad idea, if you ask me."

"Has Mason asked you?" Cora wanted to know.

Lily threw her mother a scowl. "Asked me what?"

"To marry him."

She shrugged. "No. Yes. Well, kind of. He put it in the form of a business deal."

"To settle your debts?"

Lily turned, leaning back on the rail, her eyes centered on her mother's amused face. "Yes, he wants to pay off my debts. He said he'd either buy back the place or we could get married. It's...it's all so crazy."

"Then take him up on it," Cora suggested calmly.

"The marriage?"

"No, let the man buy you out. Maybe he wants that land back in his family, after all."

"He says he doesn't want it," Lily replied, wondering why her mother was taking all of this so much better than she was. "You know as well as I do that Mason has no desire to ever come back to Caddo Lake."

"Too many bad memories."

"Exactly."

"And you—don't you have bad memories, too? Do you really want to stay on that place?"

"It's my home now. I've had good times there as well as bad."

She wouldn't tell her mother that the loneliness and the depression were starting to get to her. She'd never admit that lately, she'd been wondering what it would be like to live away from the lake, maybe in a big city such as Dallas. Just silly daydreams, nothing more.

But Cora could see right through her daughter's noble denial, as always. "You're willing to live there, alone, for the rest of your days?"

Exasperated, Lily threw up her hands. "I haven't thought that far ahead. Right now I'm just trying to make some simple decisions—such as how to pay the bills."

Cora swung her sandaled foot back and forth, one leg thrown over the other. "Sounds like you have two pretty good options. Sell out, or get married. Either way, you'd be financially set. That's a good spot of land, in a prime location. You could name your price. Mason can afford it.''

"Mother, what has gotten into you?''

Cora glanced up, shrugged, then took a long sip of her tea. "Not a thing. Except…well, there's always been something there, between Mason and you. Maybe now's a good time to find out what it is.''

Shocked, Lily groaned out loud. "I've only been a widow a little over a month now. I'm not ready to get involved with anyone, let alone Mason. I came to you for advice and now you're telling me… What exactly are you telling me?''

"Mason would make a fine husband—that's what I'm telling you," Cora said, her dark eyes lifting to meet her daughter's amazed expression. "And…the man has a thing for you, Lily. He always has.''

"I don't know what you are talking about," Lily replied, her heart beating a new rhythm. "Mason and I grew up together. He's my brother-in-law. Of course there's something between us. We're family.''

"Yes, and Mason always did run after you. I remember when the two of you were younger. You were like two peas in a pod. Fishing, swimming, going up and down this lake without a care in the world.''

Lily nodded, the memories surfacing now with an all-too-bright clarity. "Yes, and Daniel was usually right there with us. I fell in love with *him*, remember?''

"Oh, I remember that part real well," Cora replied, her tone dry. "Seems to me that happened after Mason up and left. Went off to work his way through college, left you stranded here. What choice did you have, but to marry his older brother?"

Lily threw up both hands. "I married Daniel because I loved him."

Still, her mother had a point. She'd been as close to Mason as a person could be, same as with Daniel. But that was different. She'd been a kid, tagging along with two older friends. Then she'd grown up and watched Mason go off to college, leaving her here with Daniel. It did make sense now that she'd married the one who'd seemed the most interested, the one who'd been available and willing to stay here on the lake. Shocked at the turn of her thoughts, she told herself she'd married Daniel out of love, not because Mason had left. That notion was ridiculous, almost as ridiculous as Daniel's final request.

"You don't know what you're talking about," she told her mother, but she didn't sound convincing, even to herself. And she didn't want to admit that her mother had a point. What did it matter now, anyway, after all these years? She'd made her choice and she'd been content with it.

"All I know is what I see with my own two eyes," Cora replied. "And whenever Mason Winslow is around, his eyes are usually on you."

Her gaze searching her mother's face, Lily thought back over the few times Mason had visited with her family. Neither Daniel or Mason had ever been real social, but on occasion throughout the years, they'd come over together to the Nortons' for a fish fry or a crawfish boil.

"You're wrong. He was probably just uncomfortable with all of us and so...he sought me out...since he knows me so well. I mean, Mason isn't used to a large, loving family and our family can be a bit overwhelming."

Even as she spoke, her dark-haired, big-boned brothers stood laughing and shouting to a passing boat full of neighbors having fun out on the lake. Now in semiretirement, the Nortons were known all over Caddo Lake and were a well-respected force in the community. Besides Lily's immediate family, her father had two brothers living on nearby land, each with their own large families. Lily was proud of her family, proud of the love and support she'd always been surrounded with. Daniel and Mason had never had that.

Maybe that was why Daniel had been so gentle and trustworthy, and a bit demanding—he wanted to please everyone since he thought he'd never pleased his father. But Mason—Mason had shut the world out and made his fortune his own way. Now he didn't have to answer to anyone. Yet, he probably still felt like an outsider at times.

"We obviously make him feel uncomfortable," she told her mother, referring to Mason. "Naturally he'd be more casual with me. He's known me for so long now."

"If you want to believe that," Cora said, then shrugged again.

Lily knew that shrug so well. Her mother always said so much with her body language. "So, based on Mason making eyes at me on occasion, you think I should just up and marry the man?"

"I didn't say that," Cora replied tartly. "I believe Mason would be a good husband for any woman. He's successful, dedicated and…available. And the man's asking you to marry him. Granted, it's not roses and chocolate, but then a lot of marriages have been made on lesser stuff."

Lily didn't miss the implications of that statement. Her mother had often questioned the strength of her marriage to Daniel. Especially when Daniel started changing right before their eyes. He'd been trust-worthy and gentle, all right, but…it had become a force of habit in the end. Because he was so honorable, he'd been dedicated to Lily, even if he'd stopped loving her. His dedication had become over-bearing and unreasonable at times, as if he were constantly doubting her and testing her.

She wouldn't go through that again, ever. Even if Mason did make her feel so safe and secure. It was wrong to even consider these strange, wayward feelings for her brother-in-law. Which was why she had to convince her mother that this was a very bad idea.

"But Mason would only be doing this out of some misguided sense of duty—we both would," Lily told her mother. "It wouldn't be right."

"Maybe he's trying to honor his brother's request," Cora replied.

"And you think I should, too?"

Cora got up then, her expression serious. "I think you should give it careful consideration, based on a lot of prayer and thought. As you said, you and Mason have always been close. It's only natural that you'd turn to each other now."

"How can I be sure, though?" Lily asked. "How can I just up and marry Mason? It'll look like we had lust in our hearts even when Daniel was alive, that we were secretly carrying on behind his back. What would people think?"

Cora looked out at her two sons and her husband, then turned back to Lily. "People will think what they want, but those who know you will know that you honored your first marriage in every way. And that Mason never once did anything to disgrace you or his brother."

Lily nodded, secure in that comfort at least. She'd never once considered Mason anything but a dear brother-in-law and a good friend. Until now. "But still, I just don't know if we should rush into this. How can I marry someone who's like a brother to me?"

"Honey, remember when I found out I was going to have another baby, at age forty, that your father would be changing diapers at age forty-seven?"

"Of course," Lily said. "We were all in shock for a while there, but then I was so excited to be finally getting a brother or sister."

"Yes," Cora replied, her eyes glowing. "Then when we found out it would be twins, things got a little scary. But we went on faith and we put our trust in God. We didn't question this gift, this miracle, this second chance. We just asked God to show us the way, regardless of the outcome."

Lily's gaze moved from her mother's loving face to the sight of her two rambunctious brothers wrestling to see who'd get thrown in the lake first. She'd been a preteen when the twins were born, and selfishly, she'd worried that they'd ruin her life and be a tremendous burden and inconvenience on everyone. Now she had to wonder how she'd ever lived life without them before, especially since babysitting them through the years had brought her comfort when she got depressed about not being able to conceive.

No, it hadn't been easy. Her mother had had to stay in bed the last two months of the pregnancy, but they'd all survived. And the whole time, they'd had prayer and the strength of God's love on their side.

"We don't question gifts," Cora explained. "Even when we don't understand what God wants for us."

Lily sighed long and hard. "But Mother, how can I be sure this is a gift, a second chance, as you called it? This is very different from you having the twins."

"Not so very different," Cora pointed out. "You could call it a monkey wrench, a curveball, whatever, but you've been given a choice, a way around your problems.''

''Don't look a gift horse in the mouth?''

Taking one of Lily's hands, her mother patted it fondly, an understanding smile playing at her lips. ''You can't make it here on this lake by yourself, honey. You're already too far gone financially to pull yourself back up. Stop being so stubborn and weigh all your options. If in your heart, you don't want to sell that land to Mason or anyone else, then you're gonna have to come up with some other plan—or you're gonna lose it anyway. Wouldn't it be better to let Mason have it than some stranger?''

Her mother sounded just like Daniel, declaring he wanted his widow to marry his brother rather than a stranger. Was she really so helpless that everyone had to push her off on an unwilling relative?

''Fine, then,'' Lily said, defeat draining her words. ''I'll call Mason and tell him he can have his land back. All I'll ask is that he pays off my debts and lets me stay there. That's all I really want, anyway.''

''Are you so sure about that?'' Cora prodded.

''I thought you'd be pleased,'' Lily countered, utterly confused by her mother's strange attitude.

''I'm not the one who has to make this decision,'' her mother said. ''I want you to do what your heart is telling you to do.''

''My heart is too tired to tell me anything, Mother.''

''Then maybe you should listen to Daniel's request instead," Cora said softly. "Maybe he knew in his heart what your own heart couldn't reveal."

Tears welled up in Lily's eyes. "Oh, and what's that?"

"That you have feelings for Mason, same as he has feelings for you."

Lily shook her head. "There you go, being silly again. I can't believe my husband would actually condone this relationship, especially if he thought the vows I took with him were false. Mason and I are close, but it's not what you think."

"It doesn't matter what I think," Cora said. "What matters is how you feel about the man right now, today."

Lily gritted her teeth, then took a long sigh. "I care about Mason, of course. But I'm not ready to rush into marriage again—that's how I feel. I just lost my husband, and I'm tired and soul-weary. I won't rush out and settle for...a loveless marriage." She stopped, then gazed at her mother. "Why did Daniel even have to suggest this?"

Her mother gave her that age-old look that told her to use her brain. "Maybe Daniel wasn't making a request so much as he was giving you his blessing. Maybe this is his way of finding redemption—by offering you the gift of happiness that he knew he could never give you. Maybe he saw something there that the two of you didn't."

"Oh, Mama." Lily fell into her mother's open arms. "I don't know what to do."

"Pray about it, sugar. You'll find the answer soon."

"It had better be soon," Lily said. "Or I will lose everything."

Including Mason, her heart shouted.

I could lose her.

That one thought coursed through Mason's brain as he sat at the head of the shiny glass-topped conference table located on the top floor of Winslow Industries. Outside, the Friday-afternoon rush-hour traffic zoomed by, the cars far below scurrying like colorful bugs to reach their destinations.

Always rush, rush. That was life in the big city.

"Mason?"

His executive assistant, Pam Edison, tapped him on the arm to get his attention. "Did you have anything else to say?"

Looking around, Mason saw the expectant faces of his management team, waiting for the go-ahead on their next construction project.

"I'm sorry," he said now, his attention pulled back to the matter at hand. "Wool-gathering, I guess."

Pam gave him an indulgent smile. "That's okay, boss. Even you are entitled now and again."

Mason cleared his throat and glanced down at the thick folder laying in front of him. "Yes, well, I can't afford to daydream. This hospital project is massive—one of our biggest undertakings yet. Is everyone in agreement that we're up to this?"

Robert Webb, Mason's vice president and right-hand man, nodded. "Mason, everyone knows Winslow Industries is the best at what we do. That's why we were able to snare this job in the first place." Giving his friend and boss a quick appraisal, he asked, "Are you sure *you're* up to this?" Glancing around the room, he added, "You just lost your brother. We'd all understand if you needed more time—"

"I'm fine," Mason interjected, clearly uncomfortable with the intimacy of the conversation. "But thanks, Bob." He looked up then at the many faces of the dedicated team that worked for him. "And if I haven't told y'all already, I really appreciate the cards and flowers and the donations to cancer research that you all gave in my brother's name."

Everyone nodded as the room became quiet.

Wanting desperately to lighten the mood, Mason stood up. "Hey, we just landed a major job. Let's go out and celebrate. How about steaks at that fancy joint just up the interstate—my treat."

Everyone cheered at that suggestion. Glad that he'd veered his well-meaning staff away from pitying him, Mason smiled over at Pam. "Why don't you come along?"

"I just might," she answered, her blue-green eyes centered on Robert.

"Count me in," Robert said to no one in particular.

Mason had to grin. His two best employees and two of the best friends a man could have, both single, both lonely, had only recently discovered each other.

Pam had been engaged for a while, but the relationship had gone sour when she realized the man she loved would never settle down and marry her.

Robert on the other hand, blond and good-looking, had been dating every available woman, from a Dallas cheerleader to a brain surgeon, and still hadn't found that special one to share his life with.

Until now.

Envying the way Pam and Robert huddled together near the doorway, Mason once again thought about Lily.

Lily.

Why couldn't he get her out of his mind?

Since the day that cowboy lawyer had read the stipulations of his brother's will, something had shifted and changed within Mason's hard-core shell. How could that be? How could just the seed of being married to Lily have grown into a full-fledged garden of wonderment and awe?

A garden that he wanted to explore.

But did he want this for all the wrong reasons?

Apparently, Lily thought so. Each time he called to check on her, she grew more and more distant. And she sounded tired. Probably because she was working herself to death trying to keep up that bait shop and tour business.

Daniel had barely made ends meet; how did Lily expect to be able to continue all by herself?

If anyone could do it though, it would be Lily. She'd do it on a wing and a prayer.

Mason shook his head. He'd just committed his company to a multimillion-dollar construction project, based on facts and figures and projections and long-range plans. He had always worked from a plan, and always, always, he'd made room for a back-up system of checks and balances, of research and analysis. Throughout his career, he'd never once gone on faith alone. It just wasn't in his nature.

But Lily survived on that somehow.

Not for long now though, by his calculations. She'd sold off just about everything but the house and a few essential contents. And the bait-and-tackle shop was barely holding on. Somehow he had to convince her to marry him, so he could take care of her. That was the excuse he gave himself anyway.

But in his heart, after careful consideration and lots of late-night analysis, he knew, he knew, he wanted Lily to be his wife for purely selfish reasons.

He'd lost her once, to his older brother. He could admit that now. He'd run away to find his fortune, smug in his assumption that Lily would be there waiting for him when he returned. Only, she hadn't waited, because she'd believed he didn't really want her after all. And so he'd lost her, and in his typical way, he'd accepted that as just his luck, pure and simple. Mason had stood back and allowed Daniel to claim her and take care of her, because for the longest time he'd believed them to be happy together. Well, now he knew that hadn't been the case, and now he didn't want anyone else to claim her. And he knew he was the only one who could take care of her from now on. Just as Daniel had apparently known all along.

"Hey, you're doing it again," Bob said from behind him, causing Mason to spin around.

"What?"

"Daydreaming, wool-gathering." Bob shrugged. "Call it whatever you want, but I've never seen you like this before. I'm worried about you, friend. Are you sure you're all right?"

"I'm fine," Mason assured him as he gathered up his papers and briefcase. Then, thinking he owed Bob some sort of explanation at least, he added, "I've just been concerned about my sister-in-law, Lily. With all the hospital bills and other expenses, she stands a good chance of losing her home."

Bob lifted an eyebrow. "You won't let that happen, so stop worrying."

"It's not that simple," Mason replied, a tired sigh emitting from deep within his chest. "She's so sure she can pull through. I think she believes she has to do this, for my brother's memory."

"And she won't let her rich brother-in-law help?"

"You got it, pal."

"How do *you* feel about that place? I mean, you don't talk about your boyhood home that much."

"I could care less about anything connected with that spot on Caddo Lake, I assure you," Mason replied as they walked out of the plush room.

Bob grinned. "Hey, I'm convinced. Maybe you should try convincing yourself, too, though, bud."

She'd never be able to convince the bank to give her another loan, Lily decided as she sat there staring at the mound of papers in front of her. Lifting up her cup, she grimaced as the cold coffee hit her tongue. How long had she been sitting here at this table anyway? Glancing at the clock on the stove, she was shocked to see that it was well after midnight.

She'd wanted to go over everything one last time before she caved in and called Mason to tell him he could buy this land from her. That was the only sensible way out of this. Now she could see that was the *only* way out of this.

She'd simply tell him her price, a fair one that would allow her to pay off her debts. Then she'd ask him if she could stay on here, working the tours while she trained her brothers to help with the shop. That would allow her a small income, and coupled with other part-time jobs, should keep her on an even keel. And that would allow Mason to get on with his own job, away from Caddo Lake and his bad memories.

Having made that decision, Lily told herself she'd call Mason first thing in the morning. She should feel better after finally making her choice. But somehow she felt as if she were letting something precious slip away by giving in to her worries and fears.

Time for bed. Only, what was the point? Between

the caffeine and the worry, sleep would be hard to come by.

"Lord, help me," she said out loud, just to hear some noise. Never one for air-conditioning, she had all the windows wide open. Every now and then a moth would hit one of the screens, searching for the light within.

"I feel the same way," Lily said. "What am I searching for? Money to pay these bills? That would be nice. Relief from all this stress? That would certainly help."

She thought of Mason's marriage proposal again. He could take her away from all of this if she agreed to it. No, it'd be better if she just let him buy her out. Then she could cut her losses. She knew Mason would let her stay here for as long as she wanted.

But Lord, she was so very lonely.

Her thoughts went back to her conversation with her mother. Was Cora right? Was there something between Mason and Lily?

"No," she said now, her voice rising over the sound of the pewter wind chimes just outside the open screen door.

Getting up, Lily went out on the porch to stare at the hushed waters of the lake. So serene, so peaceful. So deep and mysterious. How could she ever leave this?

"Mama's wrong," she whispered into the wind. "I care about Mason and I know he cares about me, but…"

She had to stop denying what was in her heart.

The way he'd held her right here in her kitchen all those weeks ago, the way he'd told her over and over again that she'd always have him—Daniel had never held her like that, had never reassured her like that. Was it so wrong to want a little comfort, or was she just too needy right now to think straight?

Daniel had loved her in his own way, whether from duty or from the heart, she'd never know now. But Daniel had been a studious, distant man. Friendly in a quiet, unassuming way, Daniel had always been more comfortable out on the lake than around people, especially his own wife, and he'd certainly never been one for physical affection.

Mason had some of the same characteristics, yet the other night, for that brief time, she'd seen his gentle, caring side. And that had stayed with her, reminding her of their younger days. Mason had always tried to protect her, even when she didn't need or want his protection. And then one day, he'd just up and left, with no promises between them.

Was her mother right? Had she gone willingly into Mason's arms, not because he was family and a friend, but because she'd secretly longed to be there?

"No, that would be wrong, so wrong," she told herself now. Looking up at the sky, she watched the distant stars twinkling. Was there a message there for her?

"Help me, Lord," she said again, closing her eyes as the summer wind moved over her, cooling her with its healing balm. "Show me the way."

She went back inside, her bleary eyes scanning the unopened mail lying on the table. One fat envelope, from Jim Stratmore's office, caught her eye. More lawyer stuff, probably *his* bill.

"I'll read this, then I'm going to bed," Lily told herself. Settling down at the table, she ripped open the envelope. Amazed, she recognized Daniel's looping handwriting across the enclosed sealed envelope.

Jim had typed her a short, apologetic note, stating that he'd found the letter in Daniel's file. He'd forgotten Daniel had given it to him shortly before his death, requesting that it be given to Lily upon his death.

Her eyes watering up, Lily touched a hand to the envelope where her own name called out to her in Daniel's broad, weakened scribbling. Then she carefully opened the letter.

Lily,
By now you know the final stipulation of my will. I hope that you and Mason are already married, or at least considering it. I want you and Mason to be together, Lily, but I know you. You'll be stubborn about this and think it ain't right. Look, honey, we gave it our best shot and I did love you. I do believe you loved me, too. But I often wondered if Mason had come back and asked you first, would you have gone away with him? Now's your chance. And don't feel bad about me.

We can be thankful for our time together, and know in our hearts that we had some good times. I wish I had been kinder to you, Lily, but it was hard for me to say what was always in my heart. I wish we could have had a child, but that wasn't in God's plan. Marry Mason. He'll take care of you. He promised me that much. Maybe then you can have the child we were never able to have together. Maybe then you can find some happiness at last. Do this one thing for me, Lily. But not just for my sake—Mason needs you. Please.

It was signed with a big *D*.

Tears blurring her eyes, Lily ran back out onto the porch to gulp in some much-needed air. Had even her own husband seen what she couldn't see herself? Had she married the wrong Winslow brother?

Mason needs you.

She stood there, gripping a post for support, her grief so intense, so full of a wrenching physical pain, that she thought she might surely die from it. All this time she'd believed she'd been grieving for Daniel. But she'd been grieving for so much more. She had loved Daniel and he had loved her. No, it hadn't been a great, passionate love, but it had been abiding and mutual. Yet, deep in her heart she was grieving for what could never be—just as Mason had accused her of doing.

And now Daniel had only one request of her.

Only one request, yet that request was the greatest gift he could ever give her, and also the greatest punishment she could ever receive. Daniel had given her hope again, but her guilt far outweighed that hope. What should she do with that gift and that hope? Just turn away from it because she wanted to punish herself for not loving Daniel in all the ways a woman should love a husband? Or should she relish it, cherish it, use it for some good in her life?

She straightened, wiped her eyes, then looked out over the waters that had sustained her all of her life. The darkness cloaked her, taking her in its arms to rock her to a gentle calm while the night creatures sang out to her.

Just then the phone rang, causing her to jump like a fidgety cat. "Who on earth?"

Thinking it was probably a wrong number this late at night, she slammed open the screen door, then rushed to pick up the receiver. "Hello?"

"Were you asleep?"

Mason. Her heart thudded like one of those beautiful gray moths caught against the window.

Finding her breath, she said, "No, just taking in the night air out on the porch. I...I couldn't sleep."

"Me, either." He paused, took a deep breath, then began with what he had to say. "Lily, I've been thinking—"

"Me, too," she replied, everything suddenly crystal clear in her mind. Call it loneliness, call it insanity, call it being honorable to her husband's memory, but she'd just made her decision, for better or worse.

"What?" He held his breath. She could almost hear his wonder and his worry.

"I'll do it, Mason. I'll take you up on your offer."

"You mean—to buy you out?"

Her breath caught. "No, your other offer."

He was silent, then asked, "You'll…you'll marry me?"

"Yes, that is, if you still want to go through with it."

Chapter Five

Mason held the receiver close to his ear, his gaze shifting to the moonlight flowing into his ceiling-to-floor bedroom window. Did he still want to go through with this?

What a crazy question. What a difficult question to answer. His rational side told him, no, he didn't want to go through with this. But his heart, his soul, raged at him to tell her yes, he did want this. And that was the part he didn't understand.

He'd called out of the blue, on an impulse, just to hear her voice, to see if she might have softened even a fraction toward the idea, even while he still told himself it was a crazy, impossible situation.

And now Lily was telling him she wanted to marry him.

"Mason?"

He heard her voice lifting out over the wire, heard

the doubt and the confusion in the way she said his name, felt that same doubt and confusion boiling inside himself.

"I'm here," he managed to reply, awe and wonder still causing his heart to race way too fast. "I'm sorry, Lily. You just threw me for a loop."

"You don't want to do this, do you?" she said, a long sigh emitting across the time and distance between them. "It's all right. I just got this silly notion—"

"No," he said, sitting up to run a hand through his hair. "No, Lily...I mean, yes. Yes, I still want to marry you. I just thought you'd be too stubborn to ever agree to it."

The silence stretched, bringing with it a stillness that made him tense up. "Lily?"

"Well, I changed my mind. I do want to get married," she stated simply. "I just got to thinking and...if Daniel wanted this, then I think I owe him that much at least."

Mason didn't know why her words caused him to grip the phone so tightly that his fingers hurt. Or maybe he did know and wasn't ready to admit it. "So you're marrying me strictly to honor my brother's wishes?"

Another sigh. "I'm marrying you for lots of reasons, Mason. I care about you, and I want you to have your land back. I think we could be good for each other. And yes, because Daniel wanted this."

"At least you're being honest," he said. Could

he be equally as honest? Should he tell her now that he didn't want children, that he was relieved she couldn't conceive?

No, better to let that be for now. He didn't want to rub salt into her wounds.

"I believe we should be honest," she replied. "We can go into this with our eyes wide open, knowing that we're honoring a request, knowing the stipulations. But we still need to talk, Mason. This is a big step, one that I don't take lightly."

He understood what she was saying. Lily would make a solemn, complete commitment to him. And she'd expect him to do the same for her. Because of that, they had to be very sure.

"Well, I don't want to talk about this over the phone," he told her. No, he wanted to see her face, her eyes, when he formally asked for her hand in marriage. "I'll drive over first thing in the morning. That'll give us the whole weekend to plan this out."

"Okay." Lily touched a hand to her throbbing temple. It all sounded so clinical and businesslike, but then, what else could she expect? Mason was only being a dutiful brother. She had to remember that.

And she hadn't been completely honest with him. She hadn't told him about Daniel's letter. If she told Mason that Daniel thought Mason needed her in his life, Mason would bolt. And she certainly didn't intend to tell Mason that Daniel believed the two of them could have a child together. That, of course, was impossible since she couldn't conceive. This marriage was a marriage in name only, but she intended to be a good wife to him.

Still feeling unsure, she said, "I guess I'll see you at breakfast, then."

"Blueberry pancakes? You do make the best blueberry pancakes."

"Of course, and lots of strong coffee."

"We'll need that. Somehow I don't think either of us will be getting much sleep."

"No," Lily agreed. "Good night, Mason."

"Good night, Lily."

After she put down the receiver, for some strange reason she felt more at peace. Finally making a firm decision had perhaps set her on a better path. She'd agreed to this; now she didn't want to talk herself right out of it. She would honor Daniel's request by honoring her commitment to his brother.

Once again she looked out into the tranquil night. "Okay, Lord, I've gone and done the deed. Please show me the way. Please let me be the best wife I can for Mason."

And let him be a good husband, she added silently as she wrapped her arms across her chest and remembered how he'd held her so tenderly just a few weeks ago. With that memory in her mind, she went to bed and finally found some blessed sleep.

Her peace and calm disappeared, however, the minute Mason pulled up in her driveway, the bright morning sun reflecting like a beacon off his shiny black car.

"I must be crazy," she hissed to her reflection in the hallway mirror. "Must have been that full moon last night."

Why else would she have blurted out to him that she wanted to marry him. Poor man. Now he couldn't—no, he wouldn't—back out, simply because of that Winslow honor that their mother had instilled in him and his brother.

Reminding herself that one of the reasons she had for doing this was so that Mason would automatically inherit his land back, she smiled and waved. Brushing a sweaty palm over her gathered denim skirt, she walked out on the porch.

"Coffee's ready," she said by way of hello. "And the pancake batter is all made up. Just have to throw it on the griddle."

Mason, suddenly seeming as nervous and tongue-tied as a sixth grader, managed a bright smile. "You'll spoil me, you know."

"I intend to spoil you." The words were out before she even thought about the implications.

Mason watched as she felt the blush creep over her face. He looked a little flushed himself. "This is awkward, isn't it?" he asked.

"I'll say." She turned to go back in the house, holding the door until he caught it and held it for her instead. "You can still back out if you want."

Once inside, he pulled her around to face him.

"I've had enough time to think about this, and I don't want to back out."

Lily's breath caught at the warm look in his deep blue eyes. Full moon or not, any woman would be lucky to be this man's wife. "I…I just want this to work, Mason. I don't want you to ever feel as if you've made a big mistake with me."

"Marrying you could never be a mistake," he told her, his hand brushing her arm in a gentle fashion. The look in his eyes changed from warm to heated, making her blush go one shade deeper.

Making her heart open another notch or two.

Wanting to get back to the teasing camaraderie they'd always shared, Lily nudged him away. "Do you want those pancakes, or not?"

"I *am* hungry," Mason said. Amused, he enjoyed the way being near him seemed to unnerve her. But he had to remember, this was all still new to both of them. Lily was just uncomfortable, nothing more.

Her back turned, she said, "I thought after breakfast, and after we've talked things through, we could call my parents. We have to tell them right away."

"That's fine." Boy, he dreaded facing down Lily's father. He'd have some explaining to do with Bill Norton. But it would be worth her father's wrath, just to know that soon she would be his wife. "Where do you want to have the ceremony?" Mason asked now as he settled down with a large mug of coffee.

Lily whirled from her steaming griddle. "I honestly hadn't thought about that. A ceremony. A wedding ceremony.'' Mason watched as the magnitude of what they were doing hit her full force. Giving him a searching look, she asked on a voice weak with doubt, ''Mason, are you sure?''

He got up to come and stand by her, one hand reaching up to cup her chin. The look in her dark eyes tore through him like a gentle storm. ''I'm sure, Lily. Are you?''

Remembering Daniel's letter, remembering her need to make sure Mason had his home place back, remembering her need to be held and needed, Lily nodded. ''Yes, I'm sure. Just a bad case of the jitters.''

Mason brushed a finger across her cheek. ''I know this is scary and kind of strange, and I'm still amazed about all of this myself, but I promise you this, Lily. I will try to honor you and cherish you, and I'll work hard to be a good husband to you.''

She shot him a look that told him she didn't expect anything beyond companionship. ''You don't make promises, remember?''

He shot her a look that spoke of a newfound intimacy and a willing commitment. ''Only promises I intend to keep.''

''Oh.'' She turned to flip the brown, bubbling pancakes, leaving his hand to trail down over her dark hair.

Leaving his heart at his feet.

* * *

"And so...after thinking about this over the last few weeks, we've...we've decided—"

Lily stopped, her gaze shifting from her father's tanned, furrowed brow to her mother's expectant face. Both her brothers stared at her as if she'd grown two heads. Looking toward Mason, she hoped for courage. He looked as unsure about all of this as she felt.

Mason saw her distress and cleared his throat to speak. They'd driven the few miles to her parents' house just after breakfast, and now here they all sat in the yard, out by the cool lake waters. Except Mason was sweating.

"We've decided to get married," Mason finished for her, his tone both defiant and definite.

A brilliant silence fell over the yard and the lake. Even the leaves on the trees seemed to come to a standstill. Then, in typical teenage fashion, Pete and Jeremy looked at each other, grinned and gave each other a high-five.

"All right!" they said in unison. A scowl from their father brought them both down to earth, but Mason appreciated the adolescent vote of confidence.

"Come again?" Bill Norton said, his dark eyes, so much like his daughter's, going wide. "Son, are you telling me that you're going to marry my daughter?"

"Yes, sir, that's what I'm telling you," Mason said, his own gaze challenging. "My brother wanted this—left it as a final request in his will. So Lily and I have decided to honor that request.''

Cora remained silent, her gaze sweeping her daughter's face, her arm restraining her shocked husband.

"Six weeks after Daniel's death, you two just up and decide to get married!'' Bill scratched his salt-and-peppered head, then pinned Mason with an angry-father glance. "Do you think that's wise?''

"We think it's the best thing, for both of us,'' Mason explained. He wouldn't be bullied by Bill Norton. He respected Lily's father, knew him to be a fair, decent man. He was banking on that fairness and decency now, and hoping against hope that he didn't suffer a broken nose, brought about by Mr. Norton's meaty fist in his face.

Bill nodded his head in a slow, measuring fashion, as he sized Mason up and let this information sink in. "All right. Tell me why it's best for my newly widowed daughter to turn around and marry her brother-in-law.''

Lily raised a hand before Mason could speak. "Because, Daddy, Daniel wanted this. He based his request on the Old Testament law of a man marrying his brother's widow.''

Pete and Jeremy exchanged puzzled looks.

"If I go first, I'd sure never ask you to marry my wife,'' Pete said, rolling his eyes.

"Well, first you gotta get a wife,'' Jeremy countered with a big grin. "Right now, you don't even have a steady girl."

Another glare from their confused father shut them up, but they still gave each other "whatever" glances.

"Daniel believed this would be best for both of us," Lily tried to explain.

"That's not a good enough reason," Bill interjected.

"No, it's not," Lily admitted. Choosing her words carefully, she could understand how this whole idea sounded incredible to her parents. "But we have several reasons for deciding to do this. First, it will allow Mason to get his property back—"

"I told you I don't care about that," Mason interrupted, his gaze shifting to her face.

Bill, however, seized on that notion and ran with it. "Are you so sure? That's a prime spot on a popular lake, son. Tourists coming and going, people willing to pay just about any price for that view. And you being such a savvy businessman and all."

"I will never sell that land," Mason said through gritted teeth. "It will always belong to Lily. In fact, I told her this morning I'll have papers drawn up to that effect."

"That's mighty big of you," Bill replied, doubt and accusation clear in his eyes.

"Okay," Lily said, sighing. "We won't argue

about the land. For now, it's still in the family, both families.''

"So why else should you marry him?'' Bill asked, his fists clenching tightly as he eyeballed Mason.

"Because we care about each other,'' Lily stated on a quiet, calm voice. "Because I can't stay in that house alone anymore.'' She stopped, her voice hitching. "Not after—''

Cora spoke at last. "Not after having to watch Daniel die there, not after all the pain. Is that it, honey?''

"Yes,'' Lily said, grateful that her mother could stay levelheaded about this, at least.

But her mother's next words only added to her woes. "Is that a good reason to marry someone, though? Just out of loneliness and pain?''

Lily thought about that, then said, "It's more than just that. I've really thought everything over and I believe I can be a good wife to Mason, and I know he'll take care of me.''

"Not that she needs taking care of,'' Mason said, his gaze warm on the woman at his side. "Lily is a very capable woman.'' To prove his point, he added, "She's already saved money by selling off some of the smaller equipment that…that she can't use now that Daniel is gone, and she's done a good job with the daily tours and the bait shop.''

"Yeah,'' Pete said, bobbing his head. "She's even teaching old hardhead here—'' he glanced at his brother "—and me all about running that place."

"I raise my children to be responsible, dependable adults," Bill said with just enough smugness to let Mason know that he didn't like this setup, not one little bit. "So why's she got to up and run off with you?"

"'Cause he's almost as rich as Donald Trump," Pete offered, then hung his head at his father's glowering look.

"Money can't buy peace of mind," Bill told his son, his eyes still on Mason.

"But it sure can buy a lot of stuff," Jeremy told them, his grin as wide as the curve in the lake. "Hey, Mason, I hear you've got your own plane—a Cessna, ain't it?"

Mason smiled. "I do have a two-seater, yes. We use it strictly for business—well, most of the time. But fellows, you've got the wrong impression about me. I'm not quite as rich as Mr. Trump."

"But you're listed as one of the one hundred most successful men in Texas," Jeremy said. "Daniel told us that. He was real proud of you."

"Really?" Mason asked, surprised. "I never knew Daniel even talked about me."

"All the time," Pete replied.

Even as Jeremy asked when he could have a ride in the plane, Bill snorted. "I don't want to hear any more about your fancy toys or how much money you're rolling in. I just want to understand why you want to marry my daughter.''

Mason took a deep breath. He'd faced down a lot of executives in his day—brilliant men all, full of pompous attitudes and cutthroat arrogance. But never in his life had he had to face down someone as formidable as a worried, loving, overprotective father.

Deciding complete honesty would be best in this case, he gave Bill Norton a long, intense look. ''You know, sir, I don't understand this myself. All I know is that once my brother's request planted this idea in my head, it stayed with me. And the more I thought about it, the more sense it made. At first, Lily refused to even think about it and I had to agree with her, but then—'' he stopped, looked over at Lily, his voice going soft ''—then I realized my brother loved me enough to want me to be happy. Lily is an incredible woman, Mr. Norton. What man in his right mind wouldn't want her as his bride, as his wife?''

Something in Bill Norton's expression shifted and softened. He started to speak, but at a warning look from his smiling, teary-eyed wife, he thought better of it.

His son Pete didn't have the good sense to keep quiet, however. ''Gosh, Mason, it almost sounds as if you're in love with her.'' Giving his sister a quizzical glance, he looked as if he were trying to figure out how that could happen. ''I mean, I love you, sis, but…hey, you do look real pretty, though, sitting there making goo-goo eyes at Mason."

His teasing grin shifted to an apologetic expression, however, when his father put a firm hand on his arm. "Sorry."

Mason pulled his gaze away from Lily's lovely, blushing face, realizing he'd come very close to making a complete idiot of himself. "I do care about your sister," he told Pete. "A whole lot."

"Then it's okay by me," Pete said, shrugging. He got up then and patted Lily on the arm. "Great, sis." Then he leaned close. "Can we come and visit at the condo in Corpus Christi?"

"Gabriel Peter," Cora said, her expression hard on her adorable son. "Take Jeremy David and go finish that yard work out by the road. Now."

"She used our given names," Jeremy told his brother. "And it's your fault, dummy."

"Is not," Pete replied, slapping his brother on the arm. "You started it."

"Now," Cora replied in a stern, no-nonsense voice.

Mason grinned as the two gangly teens laughed and whispered in hushed tones. No doubt debating which of his so-called toys they wanted to try out first. The hostile, disapproving look Bill Norton shot him brought his grin to a more serious measure, however.

"I'm still not so convinced," Bill told him once

the boys were out of earshot, the dare in the words as clear as the blue Texas sky over their heads.

"Then, maybe this will convince you," Mason replied. He had planned on doing this when he and Lily were alone again, but decided it might have more impact right now. Pulling a small black velvet box out of the pocket of his khakis, he searched Lily's face. His eyes on hers, he got up from the wrought-iron patio chair to kneel in front of her.

"Mason?" she said on a breathy whisper, clearly confused by his actions. "What are you doing?"

Mason ignored her question, then on bended knee, opened the ring box to reveal a brilliant diamond solitaire, encased in a filigreed band. "I made the jeweler open at dawn so I could get you this," he explained. "Lily, will you marry me?"

Lily glanced down at the bright, multifaceted ring centered on the blue velvet. She certainly had never expected anything like this. To his credit, he hadn't been overly extravagant. It was a simple ring, almost old-fashioned with its gold etchings and small diamond. Still, no telling how much he'd paid for the thing. But oh, how beautiful it looked in the morning light, like a star swirling amidst gold ribbons, calling to her, beckoning to her. And how very sweet and thoughtful that he'd chosen a ring to suit her—not too flashy or overpowering. She wouldn't cry; she refused to cry.

Glancing up at her parents, she gave them a

pleading look. Cora smiled, then dabbed at her eyes. Bill glowered, but his eyes were suspiciously misty.

Finally her father spoke in a gruff voice. "Take the man up on his offer, daughter. Just remember, bright shiny baubles don't make a marriage strong. It's the bright shiny love inside that makes a marriage."

With that, Bill got up and stalked away to his boat. Cora gave Lily an indulgent smile, then rose to follow her husband. "He'll come around, honey."

Lily didn't reply. She couldn't speak. She could only sit there looking down at the man kneeling before her, the echo of her father's parting words shouting through her mind.

Mason took her hand to place the ring on her finger. "Well, say something, please."

Finally she found her voice. "I've already told you I'd marry you. You didn't have to do this, Mason."

"Yes, I did. I want this to be right, Lily."

She nodded, admiring the ring. "And what about what my daddy said? What about love, Mason? That's the one thing we haven't considered in all of this. What if we can't make it work, because we don't love each other?"

Chapter Six

Mason pondered that question over the next couple of weeks, while Lily and her mother planned a simple ceremony to be held at the little chapel located on the lake near her parents' home. He'd never really answered Lily's question that morning. Mainly because Lily herself hadn't let him.

"It's all right," she'd told him, raising up out of her chair to run a shaking hand down the front of her skirt. "You don't have to answer that. We both know this marriage is for practical purposes—companionship, friendship, to get me out of debt, to honor Daniel's request."

"Yes," he'd agreed, glad that he didn't have to delve into his feelings just yet, but not so glad that she had to be so sensible about this. "We'll just take it from there and see how things go."

"Okay."

With that, she'd thanked him for the ring, then suggested they get back to her house. They still had lots of plans to make.

And so they had done just that. But the air around them, the wind and the rain and the flowers and the trees, seemed to hum with that one question.

What about love?

"Are you sure you know what you're doing?" Robert Webb asked now as he watched Mason bring a suitcase down the winding stairs of the newly built home Mason had purchased a few months ago. "It's not too late to back out."

Mason set his suitcase down on the tiled entryway floor of the spacious yet pretty bare house, then turned to his worried friend. "Do you still want to be my best man?"

"Yes, but that's not what I asked you."

"Yes, but that's what I just asked you. I'm going to go through with this. Just wanted to make sure you were still with me."

Robert gave his friend a wide-eyed look. "I'm still with you, pal. I'm just a little confused about all of this." Pointing a finger at Mason, he said, "You were a confirmed bachelor, content to work till the wee hours of the morning, content to date a few debutantes and socialites here and there just to keep up appearances. Now you're going to marry your sister-in-law, simply because your late brother requested it? That doesn't sound like the Mason I know and love."

Mason glanced around the austere furnishings of his overpriced, underdecorated, completely lonely home. He wasn't ready to get into this with Robert, or anyone else, for that matter. "Then maybe you don't really know me."

"Maybe not," Robert conceded, worry creasing his brow. "But I do know that you never do anything without a very good reason. Look, Mase, this is none of my business, but—"

Mason patted his friend on the shoulder, hoping his grin would hide the seriousness in his tone. "You're right. It is none of your business. Now can we go? I told Lily we'd be there by noon."

"Okay, okay." Robert threw up his hands in defeat. "I won't badger you anymore. All I can say, and you know I always have to say what's on my mind, is this Lily must be one special woman. I can't wait to meet her."

"She is, and let's get going so you can do just that."

Before Robert could question him any further, he shoved his friend out the door and turned to make sure the security alarm was in place. After all, he'd paid a pretty penny for this house and this location. Wouldn't want anyone breaking into the place before Lily had a chance to see her new home.

He liked everything locked up tight. Up until now, that had included his heart, too.

"The heart necklace is a nice touch."

Lily looked from her tense reflection in the mirror, to her cousin Elaine's soft brown eyes. "Thanks. It's from Mama and Daddy."

Elaine came to stand by Lily, so they both could check the wedding dress again in the full-length mirror of Lily's old bedroom. She'd decided to get ready for the wedding here, in her parents' home. She couldn't bear being alone in her own home, especially on her wedding day.

"You look so pretty, Lily," Elaine said, her smile as soft as the sunlight streaming through the white lacy sheers at the windows. "And I'm so thrilled to be your matron of honor."

Lily clasped Elaine's hand. "I had to ask my favorite cousin, didn't I? Remember, you lived too far away to even come to my first wedding."

Elaine gave her an impish smile, then fluffed a hand through her short brunette locks. "Yep, I was out trying to find myself or some such nonsense. Well, that all certainly changed. Came home for a visit, fell in love with the owner of the best catfish restaurant in East Texas and never left again—"

"A man I fixed you up with, I might remind you," Lily said, laughing. "Although I think it was that pretty pink dress you had on when we went to Catfish Landing for lunch that did the trick."

"Yes, and up until *your* wedding announcement, I thought I had had the shortest courtship on this lake. And now, all these years later, I'm up to my elbows in catfish and four healthy, hyper children, thanks to you." She stopped, her mouth dropping open. "I'm sorry."

"For what?" Lily asked, her hand still holding Elaine's. "You don't have to apologize because the good Lord blessed you with children, Elaine."

"I know, I know," Elaine said, clearly embarrassed. "I just don't want any sad thoughts to spoil your wedding day."

"No sad thoughts," Lily told the other woman, then letting go of her hand, turned away from the mirror. Maybe she didn't want to see the darkness there in her own eyes. To change the subject, she said, "I wonder how Mason and his crew are doing."

Elaine laughed at that. "With the twins and that handsome best man of his helping, I'm sure he's in good hands." She sank down on the bed, her eyes going dreamy. "And Lily, if I haven't already told you—your husband-to-be sure is easy on the eye, honey."

"You *have* told me, several times," Lily replied through a giggle. "Do I need to remind you that you have a handsome husband named Chuck?"

Elaine batted her long lashes. "Of course not. I'm just glad you picked a good one for yourself, too. You know, Daniel was good-looking, but his brother—well, I just think it's great that you two found comfort with each other." She stopped, then brought a hand to her mouth. "Oops, I've done it again."

Lily sat down beside her, careful not to wrinkle her cream-colored dress. "You haven't done anything. And you don't have to walk on eggshells around me. I've accepted that I can't have children, and I've accepted Daniel's death. And you're right about Mason. He has been a comfort to me."

She couldn't tell her friend that, right now, she felt anything but comfortable. She was as nervous as a cricket caught in a wire bait box. But she refused to let her skittishness show. Fluffing the chiffon layers of her tea-length dress, she said, "This is a new day, Elaine, with new blessings and new challenges. I'm going to make the most of it, and be happy." *In spite of the butterflies in my stomach.*

"Well, I'm happy for you, too," Elaine said, clearly relieved. "Now, I think since you're all ready, I'll go check on the others, then head my gang out to the chapel. Poor Mason. He probably didn't realize he's not only getting a new bride, but a whole extended family, mostly boys at that!"

After her cousin left, Lily sat there on the bed, looking around at the room she'd grown up in. Lace and ribbons, stuffed animals and books, posters on the walls. Her mother hadn't changed much in this dainty room since Lily had moved out.

But oh, how I've changed, Lily thought. About to be married for the second time, just a couple of months after burying her first husband. Was she crazy?

And what about Mason?

She'd talked to him on the phone earlier today, just after he and his friend Robert had arrived at Lily's place to get dressed for the afternoon wedding.

"Hi. We're here," Mason had said.

"Hi. Did you find everything you needed?"

"Yeah. I used to live here, remember? I know where the bathroom is."

"Right. Is your friend doing okay?" she had said.

"He's as nervous as me, I think."

"Are you nervous?"

"Kinda. Just afraid your father might decide to throw me in the lake and be done with it."

"He won't do that. He's all bark and no bite, most of the time."

"And how are you?" Mason had said.

"I'm fine. Enjoying being pampered by all my relatives."

"You do have lots of those."

"And you'll get to meet every one of them."

"Lily, I..."

"What?"

"Nothing. I just can't wait to see you."

His words had given her a special glow. Mason wanted to see her. Well, he'd get his wish soon. In less than an hour. In less than an hour her life would change forever. It had already changed.

The Monday after they'd agreed to get married, all of her debts had been wiped clean. Mason had simply called the bank and told them he would be transferring a large sum of money to them, to cover any outstanding loans owed by Lily Winslow. So easy. So quick and sure.

Then he'd had Jim Stratmore draw up papers stating that the lake house and the surrounding land would always be in Lily's name—as a wedding gift to her. A gesture that had completely defeated one of her reasons for agreeing to this marriage to begin with, but a gesture that had secured her father's grudging appreciation and respect for Mason. And Lily's undying gratitude.

But Mason hadn't stopped there.

She now owned Winslow Bait, Tackle and Tours with no overhead mortgage from the bank.

Debt free. But not free, not ever free. Now she owed Mason so much more than friendship. She owed him a promise that she would be a good wife, the best wife possible. She would forever be indebted to him, because he'd already lived up to his part of this bargain, this pledge. She intended to do the same. Only, now she had to wonder just how far this marriage would go toward becoming a real one. Would Mason expect her to be intimate with him? To be a wife in every sense of the word? She'd tried not to think that far ahead, but it was hard to put it out of her mind, especially today, on her wedding day.

"Lord, am I doing the right thing? Or am I making a big mistake?"

Too late to back out now. She owed Mason her

gratitude, if nothing else. And because of that, she had agreed to move to Dallas with him. He wanted her to see his new house, to help him fix it up and decorate it. And he had promised her they would come back to the lake often, to visit and to check up on things. He'd even persuaded her somewhat-retired father, who'd been making extra money doing odd jobs and carpentry and woodcrafting work, to consider taking over the tours and management of the bait shop.

"A father, daughter and sons team," Mason had called it. And once the twins had gotten over the thought of having their gruff father as a boss, they'd agreed it sounded like a good idea.

That was Mason. A smooth operator, with the power to change lives. Lily had resented that power at first, bitter that she couldn't provide for herself without Mason's help. Now she intended to take his generosity and make it her own, in order to pay him back. Mason really didn't have anyone in his life, and he certainly didn't have the power of faith to drive him and sustain him.

Well, now it was her turn. Through God's love, she had the opportunity to change Mason's world. Now she had been given a special power of her own—the power to show Mason why he needed someone in his life, why he needed God in his life. And with God's help, she'd change things for the better, for both Mason and herself. This would be her reward; this would be her way of showing Mason how much she appreciated his unselfish gesture. It was the only way. She couldn't in good conscience live with herself if she let Mason take over all her debts, then refused to marry him.

A knock on her bedroom door brought her head up. "Yes?"

"Lily?" Her mother's voice carried through the still house. "It's time, honey. Everyone has left for the chapel. Daddy's waiting to drive us."

"Okay, Mama. I'm coming."

With that, Lily stood, glanced at her image in the mirror one more time, took a deep, calming breath, then said another prayer. "Let it be right, Lord. Let it be right between Mason and me."

But as she opened the door and followed her mother out of the house, her heart shouted the one question she had refused to let him answer, because she didn't want to know the answer. The one question she had promised herself she wouldn't think about today, or ever again.

What about love?

Mason stood inside the little cedar-scented chapel and watched as Lily walked up the aisle, her arm cradled in her father's. Taking the few seconds as an opportunity to just look at her, he was once again overcome with something akin to panic and awe mixed, something deep inside his gut, clenching like a fist, telling him that he was making the right decision, based on all the wrong reasons.

Yet he couldn't turn back now. Not when Lily looked so beautiful in her sleeveless, cream-colored dress, with her rich brown hair swept up in a becoming chignon. It was a simple dress, almost demure in its severity. The full skirt flowed out around her ankles in gentle chiffon swirls, while the fitted bodice, etched with antique lace, showed off her golden skin. Her jewelry was simple, too. A golden heart necklace with one single diamond at its center, and pearl earrings that contrasted with her dark hair and skin were her only adornments. In her hair she wore a fresh gardenia blossom, its scent lifting out all around her in a perfume as natural as the woman wearing it.

He couldn't turn back now.

He didn't want to turn back now.

So he waited and then took her arm as Bill Norton glowered a warning look at him before the big man kissed his daughter on the cheek and sat down beside her mother.

Then everything became magnified as Mason watched Lily's dark eyes. As they said their vows, promising to love, honor and cherish each other, Mason saw the flow of emotions on his bride's features, saw the trace of pain in her chocolate-colored eyes, heard the small intake of breath as she said the words that binded her to him forever.

Before he knew it, they were finished and the minister told him he could kiss his bride. Mason turned to her, his gaze sweeping her face, the glow of a hundred candles illuminating the cool, flower-filled sanctuary around them. That glow reflected in his new wife's gaze as she lifted her head to meet his, a touch of fear and expectation brightening her eyes.

At that moment, with the late-afternoon sunlight playing across her features, Lily seemed to have an aura around her. She'd never looked more beautiful, or more vulnerable.

Mason lowered his head and gently touched his lips to hers, realizing that this was the first time he'd ever kissed Lily. He wanted to savor the moment, to thank God for allowing him this chance, to show Lily that he would always respect her and cherish her. So he kissed her with a tenderness that turned to a tough, fierce brand of protection and hope, sealing their lives together in a promise to God and all witnesses.

And, to his surprise, Lily returned his kiss with a softness and a firm touching of her mouth to his, that left him breathless and…completely smitten.

What about love?

Mason drowned in her sweet lips and knew there, in that moment, he had found love. Knew that he had always loved Lily from a distance, and that now he could show her all the ways he intended to cherish her.

If she would only let him.

Lily lifted her head to stare up at her new husband, her lips parted in surprise as she gazed into his eyes. Mason's kiss had taken the breath right out of her body, making her feel both elated and afraid. Elated because she'd never been kissed in such a way before, with such a fierce tenderness, and afraid because if he kissed her like that all the time, she might manage to lose most of her practicality regarding this marriage. And her heart in the process.

By the way he stood looking at her now, with that hesitant, knowing look on his face and that deep, dark mysterious glow in his eyes, it wouldn't take much for her to fall and fall hard.

It had been hard enough, just seeing him waiting there at the altar for her, so handsome in his dark suit and crisp white dress shirt, his eyes as intensely blue as the deepest waters of Caddo Lake. It had been even harder to say the vows that would bind them together completely, with her guilt and confusion eating away at her, with this longing so deep inside her. Somehow she'd managed to get through this ceremony; somehow she would live up to the promises she'd just made.

And she would survive the sweetness of their first kiss, and add it to the treasure of memories she was beginning to store in that secret place inside her heart—a place that was now reserved solely for her new husband.

Mason dipped his head close. "Any regrets so far?"

"None," she said, realizing it was true. She didn't regret marrying him; she only regretted that she hadn't given her heart completely to his brother. She wouldn't make that same mistake with Mason, though. They were going into this with their eyes wide open, with no illusions between them.

"Then, Mrs. Winslow," he said as he smiled and presented his new bride to the small audience watching them, "I suggest we celebrate our wedding with our friends and family."

"All right," Lily replied, her smile genuine, while her heart tripped and skipped over old guilts and rehashed regrets. "I'm ready."

The reception was held underneath a large, rounded gazebo in the chapel's dainty garden. With the sights and smells of summer all around them, Mason and Lily enjoyed lemonade punch and catfish fingers and all the trimmings, courtesy of Elaine's husband and his efficient team of caterers.

Soon it was time to cut the white-frosted cake that Lily's mother had baked from scratch and decorated with every kind of flower-shaped icing imaginable. "I made it colorful, just like your garden," she told Lily as she handed her and Mason the knife.

As the sun began to set over Caddo Lake, Lily took a piece of the rich cake on a fork and fed it to her new husband.

Mason smiled down at her as he bit into the flaky yellow concoction. "I know one thing—I'll certainly eat better now that I'm officially a member of your family."

In spite of the quiet tension that had gnawed at her throughout the ceremony and reception, she had to laugh. "We've never gone hungry around here."

He lifted his eyes toward the sky. "And you're an even better cook than your mom. I'll gain twenty pounds."

"You look fit to me."

"So do you. You look much better than you did a few weeks ago."

His words froze her smile in place. "Yes, well, things have certainly changed over the last few weeks."

As if sensing her guilt, Mason took the plate of cake from her and set it on a nearby wrought-iron table. "Lily, we did the right thing. Honey, don't look so sad. I couldn't take it if you already regret marrying me."

Careful to keep her voice low, Lily glanced up at him. "I don't regret our decision, Mason. It's just so soon. I've barely had time to find any sort of closure from losing Daniel."

"And you think we rushed into this too quickly?"

"I don't know what I think. I just don't want to disappoint you—the way I did Daniel."

Mason pulled her close then, his eyes scanning her face. "You could never disappoint me. You know me, Lily. I'm a businessman. Do you think I would ever go through with something this important, if I wasn't very sure it could reap tremendous benefits?"

"Benefits?" She scoffed, then dropped her head. "You make it sound like an insurance policy or a new construction deal. Is that what marriage is all about—benefits?"

"You know what I mean," he said, his words whispered for her ears only. "A good marriage should have certain benefits for both parties. And we *can* be good for each other. I need someone in my life, to help me fill that empty house, to cook me decent meals, to be a companion. And you—"

"I needed a knight in white satin to rescue me from all my debts and from my loneliness," she finished for him, her tone bittersweet. "Maybe that's what's really bothering me. I'm not used to being rescued, Mason. I've always managed to take care of myself."

"Yes," he said, nodding his head. "You did what you had to do for Daniel, for your family. You've always been the best person you could be—for everyone else. Maybe it's time you let someone pamper you and spoil you."

"And you want to do that?"

He touched a finger to her cheekbone and Lily felt a delicious shiver moving like wind on water down her spine.

"I want to do that," he replied simply.

She stood there, cradled in his arms as dusk danced across the lake in pastel shades of coral and mauve. In the great cypress trees edging the water, strands of Spanish moss played their own lullaby.

She could hear the gentle *swish, swish* of the draping gray moss moving against the scented green of the trees as the breeze touched down, then lifted out over the gently lapping water. Across the bayou, a willowy white egret opened its broad wings and took flight to find food in the shallow marshes where creamy fat water lilies floated like scented candles over the swamp.

For just an instant, Lily savored the feeling of being pampered. It would be so nice to give in to this longing deep within her soul, to truly let Mason hold her in his arms, and not just at arm's length. Here, in this earthy setting, where God's mastery emerged in so many new and wondrous ways each and every day, she could almost believe that she belonged in Mason's arms, in Mason's life.

"Lily?" he asked, his gaze as gentle as the sun's last rays. "Will you let me take care of you?"

She didn't deserve this second chance, but she was greedy with needing it. So she nodded. "I'll try."

He smiled then, and her heart moved as if being pulled by the evening tide. Mason Winslow's smile was breathtaking, so full of confidence and...joy? What else did she see there?

Before she could ask him, one of the twins took their picture and they broke apart, laughing to cover the awkwardness that threatened to expose them.

Then a car pulled up the long, graveled drive leading to the tiny chapel.

"We have another wedding guest," Cora said as she squinted toward the vehicle. "Hmmm. Fancy automobile. Anybody know who that could be?"

Lily glanced at the gleaming white luxury sedan, watching along with everyone else as a tall but frail, distinguished-looking man got out of the car and started toward her and Mason. Turning to Mason, she asked, "Did you forget to tell me we'd be having a late arrival?"

The look on Mason's face startled her. His expression had gone from contented to furious as he stared at the man now headed to greet them.

She touched a hand to his arm. "Mason?"

"I didn't forget him, Lily," Mason said, the words grounded out between clenched teeth. "He's uninvited, and you're right, he is a late arrival. Way too late."

"What—"

Before she could question him, the gray-haired man came face-to-face with them, his stark blue eyes centered on Mason, his whole demeanor tense and questioning. Lifting a hand to encompass the small gathering of people, he glanced around. "Looks like I'm interrupting an important event."

Then he turned back to face Mason. "Hello, son."

Chapter Seven

Stunned, Lily glanced from the man in front of her to the man at her side. She'd never seen Mason so angry. From the frown on his handsome face to the throbbing pulse threading down his jawline, his rage ran as deep and swift as the lake waters around them. And it was every bit directed toward Curtis Winslow, Mason's long-lost father.

"What are you doing here?" Mason said at last.

Around them, the small crowd of people gathered to watch, silent and waiting. Even the usually noisy twins quieted and watched, their eyes wide with teenage curiosity.

"Just got back into town," Curtis explained, his gaze holding Mason's. "Went to the bait shop. Fellow there told me you were down here getting yourself hitched. Had to come and see for myself."

Lily looked up at the man who had abandoned

Mason and Daniel when they were just little boys. Tall and angular, Curtis Winslow wasn't a handsome man, but there was something regal about him all the same. He looked aged beyond his sixty or so years, his skin leathery and dark, his face craggy with hard living and no small amount of defiance. Lily figured his sons had inherited that same defiance. Which Mason proved with his next words.

"Well, now you've seen. You can go back to whatever rock you crawled out from under," Mason told him. Taking Lily by the hand, he pulled her away. "Let's go."

"Wait," Curtis said, placing a tanned, veined hand on Mason's sleeve. "Where's your brother?"

At that question, Mason whirled to lift his father's hand away from his arm, his eyes turning a midnight-blue. "What do you mean? Don't you...don't you know about Daniel?"

Curtis shifted, glanced around. "Well, no. Like I told you, I just rolled into town. The fellow watching the store didn't fill me in on much. Just gave me directions to the chapel."

Mason moved close, his nose inches from his father's. "Then maybe I should give you some more directions—to the cemetery just down the road. That's where you'll find your oldest son. Daniel died of cancer over two months ago."

The look on Curtis Winslow's face changed from questioning to shocked. Clearly upset, he reached out, grabbing Mason's sleeve again to steady himself. "What are you saying, son?"

Mason wavered for only a minute, then pushed his father away again. "I'm saying you're too late to see Daniel. He's dead. And you're too late to see me, too. Lily and I are about to leave for Dallas, for our honeymoon."

Seeing the hurt expression on Curtis's face, Lily stepped forward. "Mason, please. Can't you see...he didn't know? Your father didn't know about Daniel."

"Of course he didn't know," Mason replied, his eyes bright with pain. "How could a father know that his son was so sick he couldn't even walk across the room? How could a husband know the wife he left pined away for him each and every day of her life, until the day she died? How could this man possibly know anything about my life, or Daniel's life?"

Curtis found a chair and sank down in it, his face pale, his breath rapid. Concerned, Lily shot Mason a warning look then rushed to Curtis's side. "Somebody, get me some punch," she said to the stunned crowd.

Jeremy quickly found a fresh cup of the chilled liquid and shoved it into Lily's hand.

"Here, Mr. Winslow," she said, coaxing him to take it. "Drink this."

Curtis took the punch, then downed it in one long

swallow. "Thanks," he said, gratitude in the one word.

"Are you all right?" Lily asked, oblivious to Mason's cold disapproval.

"Yeah," Curtis said on a weak voice. "Just…just can't believe Daniel is dead. First their ma—I heard about that long ago from a friend—now Daniel. I guess Mason is right. I'm too late."

"Daniel was a good man," Lily said, not really sure how to comfort Curtis. "You would have been proud of him."

"You knew him, then?" Curtis asked, his eyes lifting toward Mason.

Glancing over her shoulder before she answered, Lily saw the frown marring Mason's face.

"Yes, she knew him," Mason said. "She was married to him for ten years."

Curtis put his empty cup on a table, then stood on shaking legs. "I see. And now she's married to you. You don't waste any time, do you, son?"

His fists clenched, Mason glared at his father. "Yeah, I've learned not to waste time fretting over the past, or things I can't change. You taught me that, *Daddy*. Because of you, I learned to take matters into my own hands and take care of myself."

Curtis nodded slowly "Apparently, you learned a few other things, too."

Lifting a hand, Mason backed away in disgust. "Look, what I do is none of your business. You don't have any say in my life anymore. I suggest you leave. Now."

"I can't do that, son," Curtis replied. "You see, I've come home to stay. So you take your new bride and head back to Dallas if you want to. I'll be just fine back at the lake house."

"I don't think so," Mason replied, his words as icy as the punch. "You see, you don't own the lake house or the bait-and-tackle shop anymore. It belongs to Lily now. And I'm sure she doesn't want you anywhere near the place."

Whirling, Lily gave him a harsh look. "You're wrong, Mason. Your father is welcome to stay at the lake house while we're away. For as long as he needs."

Mason's frown told her he didn't like that suggestion or her generosity, not one bit. "You can't be serious."

"I'm very serious," Lily said in a stubborn voice. It wasn't in her nature to turn anyone in need away. Her parents never had and she wasn't about to start now. "You gave me that land and that house. And if your father needs a place to stay, he's welcome to stay there. I'd feel better, knowing someone's there while I'm away."

Mason glared at his father, then turned back to Lily. "Do you honestly think you can trust him? He's probably just back here because he needs money or something. He might rob you blind."

Lily looked back at Curtis and saw the humiliation coloring his face. He didn't respond to Mason's accusations. Instead he hung his head, his eyes downcast.

"I'll take my chances," Lily replied, her tone soft with compassion.

Mason tried another tactic. "And what about when we come back to visit? I don't intend to stay in the same house with *him.*"

Lily didn't want to make a scene, but it was already too late for that. The whole crowd was watching them now, and listening. "Can't we discuss this later?"

"No," Mason replied in a curt tone. "I think we need to settle this here and now. I know you mean well, Lily, but this is none of your concern."

"Yes, it is," she countered. "Your father is here and I won't turn him away from his own home."

"It doesn't belong to him anymore," Mason replied, his impatience clear. "Let's just go."

Curtis held up a hand. "It's all right, little lady. I can stay in one of the cabins on the other side of the lake."

Lily looked from one man to the other. "No, Mr. Winslow. I insist you stay at your own place. Would you like us to drive over there with you, to help you get settled in?"

Curtis looked uncomfortable, his eyes touching on Mason. "It'll be hard, going back there."

"Then I'll be glad to go with you and show you where all the groceries and linens are. And I'll have my brothers bring you some things tomorrow and whatever else you need.''

''I don't need much,'' Curtis replied, his gaze locked with his son's.

''Mason?'' Lily pivoted to face her husband and saw the wrath on his handsome face. He was furious with her and his father. But she wouldn't back down. ''Are you coming with us?''

''Do I have a choice?'' he asked no one in particular.

Bill Norton stepped forward then, a triumphant smile centered on his tanned face. ''You knew she was stubborn when you went into this, didn't you, son?''

Lily shot her father a warning look. He didn't have to take such pleasure in the fact that she and Mason were already having a disagreement.

To her relief, Mason seemed to relax a bit though. ''Yes, I knew, but I guess I'd forgotten just how stubborn your daughter can really be.'' His eyes centered on Lily with enough intensity to tell her this was far from over.

''You can take that to the bank,'' Bill replied.

''Well, right now, I'll have to settle for taking Lily and my father to the lake house,'' Mason shot back.

Bill pulled Cora to him and grinned again. ''You two have a nice honeymoon, you hear.''

Mason heard all right. Loud and clear. He heard all the memories in his head, crashing and falling all over each other like an angry gale. Why had Curtis Winslow picked his wedding day, of all days, to pop back into their lives? And why was Lily being so solicitous to the man?

He stood in the center of the kitchen, watching as she showed his father where the coffee and other staple goods were located. Still in her wedding gown, she looked like a princess, and acted like a queen. Completely in charge, completely confident, friendly, laughing, concerned.

Except when she chanced a glance at her husband.

Then her eyes went two shades darker, as if she were trying to convey some sort of message to Mason. What? Did she think he should be as nice about this as her? Did she have any idea at all what she was asking of him? How could she possibly expect him to accept his father back with open arms, without any questions, without any answers?

Trying to stay patient in spite of the slow rage boiling inside him, Mason left the kitchen and went out onto the long screened porch. The dusk was humid, the night filled with crickets chirping. He could hear the gentle lapping of the dark waters against the boat dock and the murky shoreline. Somewhere in the distance, an owl hooted a melancholy song, calling out into the night.

Mason's own heart echoed that call. What had he done? This marriage was supposed to start off on the right note, and things had been almost perfect

until his father had returned. What was the man doing back here after all these years anyway?

If Mason hadn't been so angry and full of pride,
he might have asked Curtis that very question. But
then, maybe he didn't want to know the answer.
He'd waited so long for some word, some gesture
from his father. And now that he was face-to-face
with the man, none of it seemed to matter very
much.

He just wanted to get as far away from here as
possible.

Lily came out onto the porch. "He's all settled
in. I'll just go change, then we can be on our way.
Unless you want to spend a few days here with
him."

It was a subtle suggestion, but it shouted loud and
clear to Mason. Lily was ever the peacemaker, ever
the caring, gentle soul of reason. Well, that made
her a better human being than he'd ever be.

"No." He couldn't turn to face her, couldn't take
the censure he was sure would be in her eyes. "I'd
like to go home now, if you don't mind."

"Okay."

He heard the rustle of her skirt as she turned to
leave. "Lily?"

"Yes."

"Why are you doing this?"

She stood silent for a minute, then let out a long
sigh. "Because he's come back for a reason, Mason.

And he just learned that Daniel is dead. He needs us."

Mason whirled then, his heart pumping. "He's never needed me, Lily. And whatever his reason is—I don't care."

"Well, I do," she replied. "I've often wondered where your father was, what he was doing. Was he suffering, or was he happy? It's too late for him and Daniel to make their peace, and maybe that's as it should be. Daniel forgave him long ago." The look in her eyes told Mason she expected him to do the same somehow. "I'd like to think that the two of you can sit down and talk things through."

Mason stood silent, his turmoil rising like a tidal wave. She had no right to ask this of him, not tonight of all nights.

Touching a hand on his sleeve, Lily said, "Mason, people always have reasons for doing what they do. Not always good reasons, mind you, but their own reasons, all the same. Aren't you the least bit curious as to why your father left, and why he's back now?"

Mason pivoted to face her at last. "Why should I care either way? The man didn't care enough about us to even call or check on us. We were left to fend for ourselves, to scrape and claw at a living here in the swamp." His soul exploding with pain, he added, "No, Lily, I'm not curious. And I really don't care why he's come back. He'll be gone again soon enough when he realizes he can't worm his

way back into my good graces, and I refuse to give
him my money or my sympathy. Now, can we
please leave?''

Lily lowered her head, then said, ''I feel sorry for
you, Mason. You've let this bitterness eat away at
your soul and now you have no room for forgiveness
or redemption.''

''Why should I forgive him?''

''I wasn't talking about him,'' she said. Then she
turned and went back into the house.

The two-hour drive to Dallas had been stilted and
silent, the conversation as flat as the Texas country-
side along the interstate. Whenever Lily ventured to
speak to him, Mason had responded with grunts and
monosyllables. Finally she'd given up to stare out
the window at the black dirt farmland dotted here
and there with bent mesquite trees and tall pines.

Now, as they approached the town of Mesquite,
a few miles outside of Dallas, she closed her eyes
and said a prayer. *Dear Lord, help me to stay strong.
And help Mason, Lord. He's hurting so much. And
he's angry with me for interfering. Not a good way
to start a marriage.*

She'd already been nervous enough about leaving
the lake. All of her life had been centered around
that mysterious, tranquil body of water. It had been
her anchor, her retreat, her assurance that God was
in His heaven and that He'd allowed her to live on
one of His most beautiful spots here on earth. Now

she was being swept into a world that was starkly different from the one she'd always known.

Mason's friend Robert Webb, who'd been kind enough to drive Lily's car back to Dallas for them, had already described Mason's new house in glowing detail.

"It's big to begin with," he'd told her at the reception. "But kind of bare. Mason was supposed to meet with a decorator months ago, but since he's never there anyway, well…"

Well, Lily thought now, it would be up to her to manage this house Robert had gone on and on about. A big, rambling, modern house with a swimming pool and a three-car garage. All that space for one man.

One lonely, troubled man.

Lily opened her eyes to glance over at Mason. In the scant light illuminating the dashboard controls, she could make out his profile. It looked like granite. She could see the anger, the disappointment in his guarded expression. He stared straight ahead, as if his very life depended on keeping his eyes on the road.

And maybe that was the way he viewed life. Always focused, always thinking ahead to the future, instead of looking back on the past. He was ashamed of his past, ashamed that his father had abandoned him and his family. And now he tried each and every day to make up for that past by being the best at whatever he set out to do.

Including marrying his brother's widow?

Lily wanted to reach out to him, to touch her hand to his face and tell him she understood. But she had a feeling he'd slap her hand away. After all, she'd shown kindness where he didn't see any. She'd accepted his father back, when Mason hadn't even begun to accept that his father had ever left.

"Mason?" she said now on a whisper of hope.

With an effort, he glanced over at her. "What?"

"I'm sorry."

Turning his attention back to the road, he replied, "Don't apologize for being you, Lily. You are a kind, decent woman and you did what came naturally. You reached out to a stranger in need. That's an admirable quality, but if you're looking for the same in me, I'm afraid you are going to be sorely disappointed—in both this marriage and your new husband."

"I could never be disappointed in you," she told him, her fingers itching to touch him. Clasping her hands in her lap, she tried again. "We can make this work, Mason. And I was wrong to go against your wishes tonight, without considering your feelings first."

Mason didn't answer. Instead he pulled the car off the main road and turned into a vast subdivision that spoke of wealth and privilege. After a few turns, he pulled the car up in front of a beautiful brick-and-wood house with a majestic portico gracing its front entrance.

"We're home," he said, a long sigh emitting through the words.

He moved to open his door, but Lily's hand on his arm stopped him. "Mason, I won't start this marriage with anger between us. I said I'm sorry and I mean it."

He stared over at her, his face as stark and angled as the house before them. "And I told you, you might be in for a big disappointment. You probably already regret marrying me."

"No, I don't," Lily replied, a new determination kicking in. "I went into this with my eyes wide open, Mason. Now you can sit there, wallowing in self-pity and anger, or you can accept my apology and make a commitment to start this marriage out on the right note, the way we pledged in our vows to each other."

Mason sat silent for a minute, a surprised look clear on his shadowed face, then took her hand in his. "You drive a hard bargain, Mrs. Winslow."

"I play for keeps," she replied.

Mason lifted her hand to his lips, kissed it with a soft feather of skin touching skin, then dropped it back into her lap. "I'm not easy to live with, Lily."

"I believe you."

He glanced over at her, his face now awash with admiration and longing. "And...you believe *in* me, too, don't you?"

"Yes, I do. I would never have married you if I didn't."

"Then I guess I have to live up to your expectations."

"Exactly."

"Somehow."

"You won't let me down."

His smile was bittersweet. "Ah, but I think I already have."

On that note he took her inside her new home, past the wide marble-floored entryway, up the curving stairs. And promptly placed all her belongings in a guest bedroom, down the hall from what he pointed out as the master bedroom.

"I thought you might be more comfortable in here," he explained as he turned on lamps and opened closet doors. "I have five bedrooms, so if this one isn't suitable…"

"It's fine," Lily said, too humiliated to look him in the eye. "I'm sure I'll be very comfortable here."

He headed to the door, as if a fire were on his tail. "Then I'll leave you to it. I'm exhausted and I'm sure you're tired, too."

"Yes, I guess I am."

"I'll see you in the morning."

"Good night, Mason."

He shut the door, leaving her in the middle of the vast, spacious bedroom. Leaving her alone and lonely.

Leaving her with little doubt that he did not want her here and that he, too, already regretted this marriage.

Chapter Eight

Lily decided her first week as Mason's wife might not exactly be a time of wedded bliss. Starting with Sunday morning.

"Mason, where do you attend church?" she asked as he entered the gleaming, sunny kitchen, his nostrils flaring at the scent of breakfast food.

The breakfast table was set in front of a large bay window overlooking the pool. Lily had woken up early and come downstairs to explore her new surroundings, especially the beautiful, efficient kitchen that would be a constant joy to her now that she was the lady of the house. Then, after locating the proper ingredients, and needing something to keep her jitters at bay, she'd made French toast and bacon.

Mason headed straight to the coffeepot. "I don't really attend church on a regular basis."

Lily let that soak in before continuing. "I'll find one nearby."

"And drag me along with you?" he asked, an amused gleam in his startling blue eyes. "And by the way, good morning to you, too."

She grinned, then settled down in one of the cushioned chairs surrounding the round table. "Sorry. I guess my mind was racing. This is all so new—good morning."

He took two pieces of the crusty toast, poured a good dollop of maple syrup on them, then looked over at her, his eyes going soft before he spoke. "Did you sleep okay?"

She shook her head. "I'll have to get used to that big room. But the bed is comfortable."

"If it isn't—"

"It's fine," she stated, forcing herself to take a bite of her food. She wondered what he would do if she told him that all night long she'd thought about him, just down the hall. Shouldn't a husband and wife share a bed together? Especially a newly wedded husband and wife? Had her actions regarding his father caused a permanent rift between them?

As if reading her thoughts, Mason said, "Look, Lily. I just want to give you time...time to get settled here, time to feel comfortable around me."

"I am comfortable," she insisted. Then she smiled. "Okay, I'm not comfortable. Not at all. I...I think I made a mess of things last night. I should

have minded my own business. It was our wedding
night after all...."

Mason watched as she left that statement trailing
between them. She blushed and looked away, out
toward the glistening waters of the well-maintained
pool.

She looked so pretty, sitting there in her white
cotton robe and matching gown. Had she planned
on wearing that on their wedding night—just for
him? Well, he'd planned a nice, quiet celebration,
with candles and music. But that had changed after
his father had arrived. Mason's whole mood had
changed after seeing Curtis Winslow again. Had he
been too harsh, too distant last night?

She would never know that he'd lain awake most
of the night, thinking about her, that just having her
here in his home was like a priceless gift. She'd
never know that he was so afraid of his own feelings
that he didn't want to act on those feelings, for fear
of losing her.

Let her think he was bitter and angry about his
father. He was. But he would never, ever, take that
anger out on Lily. Yet he used her assumptions as
a perfect cover for his real feelings.

And he so wanted to kiss her good-morning.

"You didn't do anything wrong," he said before
reaching across the table to take her hand. "This
thing between my father and me—I have to work
through it. You made me realize that. Your actions

made me see that I have to come to some sort of reconciliation with the man.''

"I did? They did?'' she asked, her brow lifting in surprise. "How will you go about doing that?''

"First I'll pray.'' He smiled then, cutting the tension lines around his eyes. "C'mon, don't look so shocked. I still do pray now and again, in spite of my backsliding ways and careful reliance on hard, firm facts—all of that is changing since a stubborn, dark-haired woman has entered my life.''

At that admission, Lily lowered her head and smiled herself, but didn't comment.

Mason loved seeing her blush, loved that fierce faith she possessed and apparently wanted him to possess, too. "My mother used to say those same words to us whenever our old car would tear up, or the refrigerator would go on the blink. We never had any money, so Daniel and I would always ask her what were we going to do. And she'd say, 'First, we pray.'''

Lily took a sip of coffee, then relaxed against the soft chair. "I like that. I wish I could have known your mother better. Seems like she was never around much whenever I tagged along.''

"No, always working. Two, sometimes three part-time jobs, just to keep that old place. By the time Daniel got the bait store and tours back to barely breaking even, she was too sick and tired to enjoy her retirement.''

"I'm sorry,'' Lily said. "It's funny, but when I

look back on our growing up, I don't remember you being poor. You always seemed to have the important things.''

"We did, I suppose," Mason agreed, nodding slowly. "We had love and our faith—or at least she and Daniel had their faith. I guess I hung back in the wings."

"No, you hung on to *their* wings," Lily said. "God's love and your family carried you when you couldn't carry yourself, Mason. That's what faith is all about."

He finished his breakfast, then dropped his fork. "I never thought about it that way."

Lily stood to clear the table, her back to him as she placed dishes in the sink. "And now I'm here to carry you, if you'll let me."

Mason got up to follow her. "I don't deserve you."

Lily pivoted. He was so near, she could smell the soapy clean fragrance from his morning shower. "Is that why you set me up down the hall from you? Is this a marriage in name only, because you don't think you deserve any real love or a real commitment from a woman?"

"Is that what you want this marriage to be?" he countered. "A real commitment, with real love?"

"Isn't that what a marriage should be?"

"Is this Twenty Questions?"

"No," she said, her gaze dropping away. "Just a couple of very important questions. But you don't have to answer them now. We've got all the time in the world.''

Mason stepped away. Maybe so. Maybe they did need time. But he was impatient. He wanted to pull her in his arms and kiss her and tell her that he was ready and willing to make a complete commitment to her. Instead he said, ''Well, we've got the whole day, at least. What do you want to do first—tour the house, or take a swim?''

''I want to go to church,'' Lily stated in her no-nonsense way, her dark gaze snagging him with hope.

''First, you pray,'' Mason said, nodding his understanding. ''I'll go change into a suit.''

''I'll meet you back down here in a half hour,'' she told him. And then she reached up and kissed him on the cheek. ''You're wrong, Mason. You do deserve all the good things in life, all the things that really matter.''

He watched as she marched up the back staircase centered just off the kitchen, her long hair flying out behind her.

''And you deserve so much more, Lily,'' he said, touching a hand to the cheek she'd just kissed. *So much more than I'm willing to give right now.*

After church and a quick stop at a neighborhood grocery store, they changed into their swimsuits and had a light lunch of fruit and salad out by the pool. In spite of the heat, a soothing breeze rustled the canvas umbrella centered over the floral-cushioned patio table. Soon, however, Mason got up and jumped in the pool, then deliberately splashed Lily as she sat soaking up the afternoon sun.

"C'mon in," he coaxed, his toothy grin as bright and inviting as the sunbeams dancing across the water. "It's not as big as Caddo Lake, but at least there are no 'gators waiting to nip at your cute ankles."

Unable to resist, Lily pulled off her cover-up, tugged at her one-piece swimsuit and dove in beside him, only to find him waiting for her when she surfaced. The chase was on as they raced from one end of the pool to the other and finally emerged, exhausted and laughing together, on the steps at the shallow end.

"It's good to see you laughing," Mason said, his breath coming in huffs. "But I think you're more in shape than me. I'd better plan on swimming more laps before work each day."

Lily tossed back her soaked hair, then punched him on the arm. "You look pretty good to me."

"Do I?" he asked, his expression turning serious, his eyes darkening.

"Well, of course." Flustered at the intensity of those blue eyes watching her, Lily could only nod. "Are you fishing for compliments, Mr. Winslow?"

"No, just want my new wife to be proud of me."

"I *am* proud of you," she said, her heart beating as hard and fast as the heated sun. Well aware of how close Mason sat on the steps next to her, she trailed her hand through the water. Then she turned serious, too. "Mason, what do you expect out of this marriage?"

"Wow, where'd that come from?" he asked, squinting up at her as he leaned back to cross his long legs at the ankles.

"I just need to know," Lily replied. "We talked about companionship, fellowship, togetherness. We talked about me taking over this house, attending functions as your wife, things such as that. But...I'm not sure I'll really have a place in your life."

Mason sat up then to grab her wrists and tug her toward him. "You will always have a place in my life, Lily."

Lily wondered about that statement. Why did she have this strong need to find all the answers to Mason Winslow? Why did she need to know why he'd really married her? A man like Mason didn't just do things on an impulse. *Patience, Lily,* she told herself now. *Patience.*

"I'll start on the house tomorrow," she said. "I'll certainly have my work cut out for me. What a challenge! And a dream. Every woman dreams of decorating such a house."

"Stop," he said, his hands still on her wrists.

"What? You don't want me to work on the house?"

"Yes, I want you to do whatever you feel necessary about the house, but I also want you to relax and stop trying to analyze me." Tugging her close, he brushed a wet strand of hair away from her cheek. "I know what I'm doing here, Lily. We made the right decision." Then he moved closer, pulling her into his arms. "And right now, I only have one request from my new bride."

"Oh, and what's that?" She hoped he couldn't hear her heart rate speeding up.

"I want a kiss."

"A kiss?" She lifted her gaze to meet his, then saw the need, the longing in his eyes. Telling herself he was just lonely, and that he probably wanted to reassure her, Lily leaned forward, happy to oblige him with a quick, feathery smack.

Mason protested that smack. "I want a proper kiss."

Hoping to lighten things and to calm her shaking knees, Lily quickly wiggled out of his arms and took off like a rocket through the water. "Well, you'll have to catch me first."

Mason groaned and took the bait. Soon he had her cornered at the far end of the pool. Squealing and begging for mercy, Lily giggled and tried to squirm away. But Mason was determined.

He got his kiss, another lighthearted peck at first. But the kiss soon turned from lighthearted to deeply pleasant as he pulled her back into his arms and gave her a proper welcoming to his home.

"Lily," he said, his blue eyes shimmering as he lifted his head away. "Lily."

A thrill moved through Lily's soul. She liked the

way Mason said her name, as if the one word meant
the world to him. It gave her hope and filled her
with a sense of peace. Daniel had never called out
her name in such a sweet way.

Thinking of Daniel immediately brought Lily out
of her stupor and filled her with a sense of remorse
and regret. She shouldn't feel this way, not so soon
after her husband's death. But she'd married his
brother soon enough, she reminded herself. She
stiffened in Mason's arms and pulled away.

"Are you all right?" Mason asked, letting her slip
by him in the water, his expression full of disappointment and concern.

"Just tired," she told him, unable to face him
with such guilt hanging over her head. "I think I'll
go in and finish unpacking."

"I'll come help."

"No, you stay and swim some more. I'll be fine."

Mason watched as she lifted out of the pool,
worry clouding his better judgment. Well, he'd certainly killed the mood. Had the kiss, which to him
had been wonderful and reassuring, scared Lily
away? He'd have to remember she was still full of
mourning for Daniel, and she was probably still unsure of Mason's motives in this marriage.

Wondering what he could do to make her more
comfortable as his wife, he decided maybe he should
introduce her to some new friends. They'd made a
good first contact at church this morning. A lot of
the members lived in this subdivision, and Mason

had to admit it had been nice to be received with open arms by people he'd only waved to before while passing through the neighborhood. But that fledgling fellowship might take a while to cultivate. Lily needed someone right now.

Climbing out of the water, Mason dried off then picked up the cellular phone from the patio table and dialed Robert Webb's number.

Robert answered on the second ring. "What's up, boss?"

"It's Lily," Mason said, careful to keep his voice low.

"Uh-oh, has the lady seen your bad side already?"

Mason laughed. "Yes, but she's going to stick it out anyway. Listen, I want Lily to make some new friends, meet some people. Can you and Pam arrange for a get-together later in the week? Maybe some of the gang from work and some of our clients?"

"Sure," Robert replied. "In fact, Pam's here having lunch with me. I'll talk to her and we'll get with you first thing in the morning. This would be a good idea, considering you got married so quickly. Kind of a reception-for-the-newlyweds-type thing."

"Great." Mason hung up, sure he was doing the right thing. Lily would feel much better once she was introduced to Dallas society. And it would do her good to get out and have some fun with new people.

And, he thought now as he gazed up at the window of her bedroom, it would keep him occupied, too. He didn't need to spend too much time alone with his new wife, because he had to give her the time she needed to adjust to this arrangement. He wouldn't frighten her or hurt her, so that meant he'd have to keep his distance, and keep that lock on his heart.

"No more powerful kisses," he told himself as he headed inside to shower and change.

The kiss in the pool, just as the kiss when they'd declared their vows, had left a powerful impression on Lily. Had Mason always kissed every woman he'd dated like that? Or, was Lily just imagining that he kissed her as if she were a treasure, as if she really mattered to him?

Silly, she told herself now as she dressed and dried her hair. Of course she mattered in Mason's life. He'd told her that, shown her that in so many ways. But she still didn't have the answers she wanted and needed to hear.

Not in words anyway. But, oh, in kisses, in soft secret looks, in the way he touched her, Mason told her much more than he wanted her to know, she was sure.

That only reminded her of her mother's words to her, about Mason having more than just brotherly feelings for Lily. Did Mason feel something more, just as Lily herself did now? If so, he'd surely hidden that something well over the years. Could that be why he'd seemed so distant, so aloof, each time he'd come home for a rare visit to the lake?

Well, his kisses certainly weren't distant or aloof.

Wrapping her arms around herself in a little hug, Lily sighed. She liked Mason's kisses. Too much.

Dropping her arms, she stared at herself in the mirror. "Why do I feel this way? Why didn't I feel this way with Daniel?"

That old guilt and frustration weighed heavily on her shoulders, causing her to shrug and slump. She had to remember that toward the end, the passion, the everyday joy had gone out of her relationship with Daniel, because of his sickness, because he'd given up hope. On his life. On her.

"I let you down, Daniel," she said, tears welling in her eyes. "I should have been a better wife."

Then she said a little prayer.

"Well, I'm here now, Lord, and I need Your help. I will be the best partner for Mason. Whether that means in all ways, I don't know. I'll have to see what happens there. Help me, Lord, to meet my duties in this marriage. Help me to know that Daniel really did want this for Mason and me." She dropped down on the bed then and added a whispering plea. "And help me, Lord, to ease this terrible pain, this guilt. Forgive me, forgive me, please."

With that, she dried her eyes, finished up in the bedroom, then went back downstairs to make notes on the house and start dinner while Mason did some reading in his study.

For better or worse, her tenure as Mrs. Mason Winslow had officially begun.

Chapter Nine

"Just give me the directions, Mason. I can find my way to your office on my own," Lily told him the next morning.

"Are you sure? Dallas is a lot different from those rutty roads along the lake."

Lily watched as he gathered his briefcase and cellular phone, readying himself for another day of conquering the business world.

"I'm sure," she told him again, a little put out by his assumption that she was a country bumpkin. "There is certainly no need to send someone to pick me up, as if I'm incapable of driving a car."

"I didn't mean it that way," he said as he stopped at the door leading to the garage. "I just worry about you. Your car doesn't exactly look reliable. I really wish you'd reconsider about buying a new one."

Lily herded him toward his own perfect vehicle. "Tell me the directions, Mason."

After emitting a long sigh, he pulled out a notepad and jotted down the directions to the downtown Dallas high-rise where Winslow Industries occupied a whole floor. Together they went over the route— interstate, exits, twists and turns. Lily couldn't help but smile. Mason was so thorough, a real details man. She supposed that was also why he was such a successful businessman. He left nothing to chance.

After he'd repeated himself the third time, telling her once again about the parking garage just off Commerce Street, she took his pen and pad, stuffed them into his briefcase and gave him a quick kiss on the cheek.

"Go," she told him, laughter bubbling from her throat. "I'll find my way and I'll be there by noon."

He didn't look so sure. "Okay, but remember to take the other cellular phone, just in case you get lost. And you have my private number, right?"

"Yes. Mason, I'll be there."

"Okay. You'll like Pam. And she's excited about meeting you. Something about wanting to shake the hand of the woman who finally hooked Mason Winslow." He gave an eloquent shrug. "And don't be nervous about this party we've cooked up. I want everyone to meet my new bride."

"If you say so," Lily replied, her confidence level plummeting. Since he'd announced his grand plans at breakfast, she'd had a strange burning inside her stomach. Nerves. Butterflies. Fear. She wasn't so sure she was ready to face hundreds of sophisticated strangers just yet.

But she had agreed to represent Mason, as his wife, at business functions. She'd just have to live up to that agreement.

Which was why she was determined to find her way downtown, on her own.

And that was just the beginning. She was itching to get this sparse house in shape, too. Waving to Mason, she turned and headed back into the kitchen to finish cleaning up the breakfast things. After another sleepless night, she would love to find a dark, cool corner and curl up for a nap, but that wasn't in her nature.

No, she needed busywork. So she scrubbed the already gleaming white tile countertops, dusted the various rooms, vacuumed the carpet in the wide, paneled den, then headed upstairs to wash the linens. Mason had told her he had a maid who came three times a week, but Lily didn't think she'd need a maid. The place practically kept itself, it was so big and empty.

No, what she needed was some advice on how to decorate this house. She didn't want to embarrass Mason, so she'd have to swallow her pride and hire a professional. Maybe Pam would have some suggestions on that.

Glancing at the clock, Lily realized if she didn't hurry now, she'd be late for the planned luncheon with Pam and Robert. And that wouldn't do. Mason would have both the Dallas police and the Texas Rangers out looking for her.

An hour later, Lily sat on the side of the interstate watching smoke roll out from underneath the hood of her economy car.

Searching for the small phone Mason had insisted she always keep near, she dialed his number. Waiting for him to pick up, she said to her dying car, "I guess the trip over here finally did you in, huh?"

It had been a good car for over ten years. Mason had hinted that she needed a new one, but Lily had only laughed and told him her car was fine for now.

"Mason Winslow."

Just hearing his voice reassured her. It was certainly unnerving to be sitting here with cars whizzing by and the noonday sun beating down with unrelenting accuracy.

"Mason, it's Lily—"

"Where are you? You're fifteen minutes late."

"I'm…I'm on I-30. My car broke down."

"What? Where? What exit are you near?"

After telling him her location, Lily hung up and waited for the tow truck and her husband to come and rescue her. She didn't like feeling so helpless, but then, she wasn't used to being spoiled and pampered, either. And she really didn't want to hear Mason's "I told you so."

He never said those words, though. Instead, he

pulled his sleek sedan in front of her sputtering car and hopped out, oblivious to the cars flying by, to come and open her door for her. "Are you all right?"

"I'm fine, just a little shaky. It's probably the radiator again. It acts up every once and a while."

"Well, not anymore," he told her as he led her to the cool confines of his waiting car. "The tow truck is on the way."

"I'm sorry," she said. Looking down at herself, she felt miserable. She'd dressed so carefully, in a floral short-sleeved sheath. The heavy cotton was now damp and sticking to her legs and arms. Her hair, once pulled back away from her face, now hung in limp strands around her temples. "And I look a mess. I got all hot and sweaty, trying to fix the thing."

"You got out on the side of the interstate and tried to work on your car!"

"Well, you don't have to roar. I'm sitting right here."

Mason held up a hand in apology. "Lily, that's not safe. Don't ever do that again."

"Mason, I've tinkered with that old car more times than you'll ever know. If it hadn't been for me being late, I could have figured something out."

"No more," he told her again, his eyes scanning the road for any sign of the tow truck. Seeing the bright red vehicle in the rearview mirror, he got out and talked to the driver. Then, satisfied that the man would follow his instructions to the letter, Lily guessed from watching the two talking, he got back in the car and zoomed out into traffic.

"We're late," Lily said, glancing at the clock on the dash. "I hope this hasn't ruined your schedule."

"Robert and Pam know the situation," he replied. "We all cleared our afternoon." With that, he gave her a little smile. "Just for you."

That made Lily feel even worse. "You shouldn't have. I don't want this reception, party, whatever it is, to be a big deal."

"Not quite ready for prime time?"

"Not quite," she admitted, glad that he understood. "Can we keep it simple?"

"As simple as inviting one hundred close friends to your home can be."

"Our home?" She braced a hand on her seat belt buckle, then stared over at him. "We're having this shindig at our house?"

He nodded. "Relax. You'll have plenty of help getting things ready. I've already had Pam call a decorator and a caterer. We all thought it might be cozier, letting everyone see where we live."

"You could have asked my opinion," she replied, that burning feeling inside her stomach increasing tenfold.

Mason glanced over at her, his expression going from pleased with himself to sheepish. "You're right. We should have asked how you felt about all of this. We can change the location if you're not happy with it.''

Not wanting to sound like an ungrateful brat, Lily shook her head. "No. Just let me get used to the idea."

"Okay," Mason told her as he eased the car into the parking garage near his work building. "No more discussion until all the party planners are sitting down over lunch. And no more scares on the highway, okay?"

"Okay," she agreed. "But...I guess I will need a ride back home."

"No problem." He grinned over at her. "I might even take you back myself."

The promise in his grin more than made up for Lily's bad hair day.

She'd never seen anything like it in her life. Lily sat in the black lacquered chair, in the private dining room/boardroom that was reserved solely at Mason's discretion, and viewed her surroundings with something akin to awe.

This particular room was Oriental in design, complete with murals of spectacular gardens and beautiful temples, all painted in a golden, shimmering array of colors that made her feel as if she were indeed sitting in a Japanese garden far away from downtown Dallas.

But it wasn't just the surroundings that impressed Lily. It was the respect and loyalty that Mason commanded from his employees. Oh, he didn't growl or snarl out demands. He simply explained what he wanted done and when, and it was taken care of in a matter of minutes by people running here and there like a line of soldier ants.

She watched now as a team of caterers brought in lunch from a local restaurant—salad, pasta, chicken, rolls and a decadent-looking chocolate dessert. Mason did have a sweet tooth. And he did like to boss people around.

"His bark is much worse than his bite," Robert told her, his expression amused as he reached to take her hand.

Grateful to see a familiar face, Lily shook his hand and laughed. "I told Mason the same thing about my father. In fact, I believe my sweet father is probably the first man to ever make Mason Winslow quake in his boots."

Robert settled down in the chair across from her. "That's because when he spoke with your father, he was talking with his heart, not his head."

"Do you think so?" Lily asked, liking Robert immediately. He was a handsome man, with a wonderful smile and clipped, sun-streaked dark blond hair.

"I do," he answered, his tone hushed. "Although I'd appreciate it if you didn't tell him I said that. He does have this reputation, after all."

"Uh-huh." Lily smiled, then giggled. "Does he drive you crazy, going over the details all the time?"

"Every single day, but hey, that's what makes him tick. Mason likes to be involved in every aspect of this operation, from hard hat to ribbon cutting."

"Exactly what is this operation?" she asked, thinking she'd better learn everything she could about Winslow Industries so she wouldn't put her foot in her mouth.

"We build industrial sites," Mason said from the doorway, his smile brilliant. "I'll take you out to one of the sites sometime."

"That would be nice," Lily said, her gaze lifting to Robert's. He was, of course, enjoying her discomfort at finding Mason eavesdropping on them. "How do you go about doing that—building industrial sites, I mean?"

"Well, it isn't easy." Mason said as he strolled into the room. He then fell back on the chair next to her, giving her a faint whiff of his clean-smelling aftershave. "It's not wood and nails. We construct the piping and machinery for such places as hospitals and manufacturing companies. It can be dangerous work, but we're proud that we meet all the safety standards at the workplace—and our record shows that."

"Okay, boss," Robert interrupted with a hand. "She's your wife, not a prospective client."

"Sorry." Mason's grin hid his embarrassment. "I do tend to go on sometimes."

"I don't mind," Lily said, enjoying the warmth in his eyes. "And I'd love to learn more."

Just then, Pam came sweeping into the room. Letting out a sigh, she, too, apologized. "I'm sorry I'm late. Phone calls!"

"Problems?" Mason asked as he got up to hold out a chair for his assistant.

"Nothing I can't handle, boss." Then Pam turned to Lily. "So, this is Lily. Hello."

"Hi," Lily said, taking in the beautiful tailored suit and expensive shoes the woman was wearing. Compared to Pam, Lily felt like a wallflower, a wilted wallflower, the way she was dressed. She'd have to add shopping for a new wardrobe to her list of things to do. "It's nice to meet you."

"You, too," Pam responded with an exuberant warmth. "I wanted to be at the wedding, but I had unexpected company that weekend—my parents."

"They dropped in to talk her out of marrying me," Robert explained.

"You two are…" Lily left the question hanging.

"Engaged," Pam finished, her eyes shining over at Robert as she showed Lily her lovely diamond ring. "And he's teasing. My parents like him."

Robert moaned. "Notice she said *like*—not *love*, not *crazy about*, but like."

"It's a start, my friend," Mason quipped. "Now, can we eat? I'm starving."

Lily watched his face, then his eyes lifted to hers in uncertainty. Like. It was a start. Mason liked her well enough, she guessed. And she certainly liked him, a lot.

Would that like ever turn to love, the real love between a husband and wife? She dropped her gaze away from Mason, then watched as Pam and Robert laughed and flirted with each other. They were in love, obviously.

And she and Mason weren't. Obviously.

Pam turned out to be a godsend for Lily. And an instant friend and confidante. After convincing Mason they needed more time to plan things together, they met with the decorator, who assured Lily they could get the house in order in the month they had before the party. Lily explained her vision of what she wanted to happen, and the decorator, Rachel Martin, set out to create that vision with prints and checks, florals and pastels.

Then Lily and Pam planned a shopping trip to search the antique malls just outside Dallas and the furniture stores all across town, looking for the perfect pieces to fill the house. Soon the preliminary plans were under way and the house was beginning to take on a cozy, lived-in persona.

"You're doing a good job," Mason told Lily one night about a week after their lunch meeting. "This house is really beginning to feel like a home."

Lily beamed her pride, and poured him another cup of coffee. They were sitting out by the pool, something that had become an evening ritual on the rare nights Mason made it home in time for dinner.

"And you're doing a passable job, trying to stay out of my way."

"Does it show—my need to always be in control?"

"Just a tad. You do seem to want to linger with the delivery people. I saw you just this afternoon, pointing those two from the antique store to the wrong part of the house."

"Well, I just thought that armoire would be perfect in the study."

She playfully slapped his arm. "And I told you, that armoire goes in the downstairs guest bedroom."

"It would make a great entertainment center in my study."

"No, we're not going to cut it up to fit your widescreen," she retorted, her smile indulgent. "It will store linens and have space for clothing and such."

"Okay, you win. Think you could find something similar for my study, though?"

"I just might be able to scrounge something up."

"Thank you so very much."

This was the way it was between them. Light banter, just like old times. Nothing too heavy, too intimate. Now and then a quick kiss here and there. Of course, they were both too busy for much else, Lily told herself.

Her eyes following the lay of the sloping backyard, she said, "Next week I start on the landscaping."

"And I can tell you're itching to get on with that."

"I do love a garden. And I intend to take this big old lot and turn it into a real showplace. That is if you don't mind."

"You're in charge there," Mason told her, his gaze sweeping over her face. "I don't do landscaping. But I trust you. You'll have the loveliest garden in all of Dallas, I'm sure."

"I hope so," she told him. "I miss my garden."

The words had slipped out before she realized she'd even said them. But she knew the way she'd said them told Mason more than he needed to know.

"Are you lonely here, Lily?"

"How can I be lonely?" she said on a light note, hoping to hide the forlorn emptiness inside her heart. "I've been busy since I moved in this place."

"I didn't ask you about being busy."

"I'm fine," she said, lifting her eyes to meet his direct gaze. "We both knew this would take some adjusting." Then she ventured into territory they didn't talk about. "But I think we should take a quick trip home soon. To check on your father."

Mason's features hardened. "I told you I don't want to associate with him."

"You could call and check up on him. I have. I've talked to him a lot over the last couple weeks. He's the one who's lonely, Mason."

"I really don't want to discuss my father. Give him a few more days and he'll be gone again."

"Don't you even want to know how he's doing?"

"No, but I get the feeling you're going to tell me anyway."

"He's helping Dad and the twins out with the tours and the shop," she said, a soft smile highlighting the words. "Isn't that great?"

"Wonderful. Just hope he doesn't take off with the cash box."

"You really don't trust him, do you?"

"Why should I?" he asked, his eyes dark and stormy with emotion and bitterness. "And why do you?"

"I just think we should try," she explained. "I mean, we up and left him there all alone, and I feel responsible for him—"

"You don't have to," Mason interrupted. "He was never responsible toward his own family, so why should you or I worry about him now?"

"Because it's the right thing to do."

Mason nodded then. "I know, I know. It's the Christian thing to do, and you want me to be more like that, right? You want me to forgive and forget."

Lily looked out over the pool. "I want you to find some peace."

"I'm at peace, sitting here with you," he told her.

He seemed sincere about that at least. Deciding she'd better change the subject, and conscious of his eyes on her, Lily tossed back her haphazard ponytail. "All right, then I won't badger you. But I want you to know I intend to keep in touch with your father.''

"Do whatever you have to do," Mason replied, a grudging admiration in his eyes. "Now, can we talk about us—I mean the house, and the gardens? Tell me more about your elaborate landscaping schemes."

Lily gave up trying to change his mind about his father and spent the next few minutes describing everything from mulch to manure. "And then, after that, we're going to work on me. I need a major overhaul."

Mason's expression changed then. "Well, don't change too much. I happen to like you the way you are."

Lily shook her head. "Jeans and T-shirts don't cut it here in the big city. I'm an executive wife now. I have to dress the part. I don't want you to be ashamed of me."

"I would never even think of being ashamed," he countered, his words holding a sweet conviction that made her smile.

"Well, you won't ever have to, if I have my way. I'm going to buy a new frock for our party."

"Good. You need to spend more time pampering yourself. You've been working day and night on this house."

"You told me I was in charge, remember?"

"Yes, but that doesn't mean you have to work

yourself into a frenzy. You haven't even had time to shop for a new car.''

"And when have *you* had the time?'' she reminded him. "I'm fine with mine now, anyway, since we fixed the radiator. It should last another five years at least.''

"And you should have a better vehicle,'' he replied.

Thinking perhaps he was embarrassed by her old clunker, after all, Lily nodded, feeling once again inadequate and sorely out of place. "I guess I'll have to squeeze that in before the party somehow.''

Mason watched as she got up and headed into the house, her head down. Now what had he said this time?

It always happened like this. They'd be going along, laughing, bonding, sharing, then *wham*, she'd get that faraway look in her eyes and then before he knew what had happened, she'd dart away to do some of her busywork. That woman could find more to occupy herself with than anyone he'd ever known. Or maybe she just pretended to be busy, to avoid spending more time alone with him.

Did she regret moving here, living with him? Did she resent having to be in charge of this house, having to play the part of the executive wife? At times she seemed content; other times she looked downright miserable. Was she upset because he refused to talk about his relationship with his father, because he refused to even talk to his father?

Maybe it's me, he thought now, his eyes scanning the enticing waters of the pool. *Maybe she just can't find it in her heart to take things any further between us, because she's not attracted to someone as ruthless and unforgiving as me.* Or maybe she was still feeling guilty about Daniel, about this hasty marriage, about everything.

Well, Mason was ready to take things further. And it was getting harder and harder to kiss her good-night every evening then walk away to his own room. But, he reminded himself for the hundredth time, he would not do anything to scare or upset Lily. Maybe in time she'd come to feel something more than brotherly affection toward him.

Maybe.

Maybe the night of the party. He had a surprise for her, a big one, for that night. Maybe once she was more settled, and felt more accepted here in Dallas, they could take things one step further and begin to make this a real marriage.

Maybe.

Chapter Ten

Maybe if she took another deep breath and said another little prayer, she'd be able to get through this night, Lily told herself as she stared at her reflection in the mirror over her bedroom dresser. She could almost see her heart pounding against the rounded neckline of her dark blue dinner dress.

Would Mason like what she was wearing? Would he be happy with everything she'd done to the house? Would he approve of the food, the candles, the music, the hundred other things she'd tried so hard to make perfect?

Would she ever measure up?

It wasn't in Lily's nature to admit failure. But it also wasn't in her nature to feel so self-conscious, either.

"That's because you stayed tucked away on that lake," she told herself as she touched a hand to her upswept hair once again. "That's because you never had any reason to want to impress anyone. You knew who you were and what you wanted from life."

Now, she wasn't so sure, about herself, about Mason and his feelings—his real feelings—for her, or about what she wanted and expected from this marriage. Now she wasn't so sure about going downstairs to meet and greet so many rich, highfalutin people.

She'd tried to look her best. From the pearls and the upswept hair, to the simple dark blue crepe fitted dress and matching strappy sandals, everything she saw in the mirror told her that she and Pam had done okay.

"But will okay be good enough?" she wondered now.

Glancing at the clock, she decided she'd have to do. Time was ticking and she didn't want to be late for her own party. And, she wanted a few minutes alone with Mason, just to catch her breath and take all of this in, without prying eyes watching them.

Feeling like Cinderella, Lily left the bedroom and headed down the winding staircase at a fast pace, until she looked down and saw the man waiting for her at the bottom of the steps. She had to stop halfway down, just to enjoy the sight of him.

Mason. Mason in a fitted black tuxedo, with his dark wavy hair crushed into place and his eyes centered completely on his wife. Mason, with all the confidence that she lacked; with all the charisma that drew her to him each and every day; with all the air of a lord of the manor.

Mason. The man she'd fallen in love with.

Mason looked up at Lily and felt that secret spot inside his heart opening and shifting and growing into something warm and wholehearted, something he was afraid to put a name to just yet.

She looked incredible. So beautiful, so regal in her simple, almost severe dress, with a three-strand rope of pearls encircling her slender neck, with her dark hair swept up in a do that only made a man want to put his fingers through it and mess it up completely.

How had he gotten so lucky? Mason wondered now as she stopped to gaze down at him, the vulnerable question in her eyes warring with her strength and inner serenity.

Then he remembered how he'd gotten so lucky. His very own brother had bequeathed his widow to the one man who'd thought he could never have her. His brother.

And then it hit Mason. Daniel *had* known. Daniel had seen what Mason had tried so hard to hide all these years.

He was in love with Lily. He'd always been in love with Lily. Admitting it left him both amazed and shaken.

Where did he go from here? How would he ever find the courage to tell her what was in his heart?

And could she ever find it in her heart to return his love?

All of these questions buzzed inside his head, even as he lifted his hand to coax her down the stairs. "Mrs. Winslow, you look incredible."

She smiled then, a wide open expression that took his breath away. "You look pretty dapper yourself."

Memories of their wedding came back to haunt Mason. He'd had such high hopes that night, and then his father had come along to ruin it all. No, Mason had ruined it all himself by being stubborn and distant, by trying to punish Lily for just being Lily.

He decided he had to come up with some sort of strategy to win her heart. A step-by-step plan, a bid to gain her respect. Starting with making amends for the way he'd treated her on their wedding night.

"You know," he said by way of initiating his new plan, "we need to get away, take that honeymoon we never had."

Surprise brightened her eyes as she took his hand and allowed him to escort her down the last step. "What brought that on?"

He walked around her, his eyes moving over her with approval, his fingers laced with hers. "Seeing you, seeing how much trouble you've gone to to make tonight a success. I'd say you need a rest, a few days off. I'll take you anywhere you want to go."

Lily lifted her brows. "How about home, to the lake?"

Except there, he thought, wondering why step one had just gone south. "Okay," he said, though the one word was squeaky with doubt. "How about next weekend?"

"Why not this weekend?"

Mason couldn't come up with one reason why not. He'd just have to see how his plans turned out tonight. "Uh…maybe we could arrange that."

"Really?" She gave him a doubtful look. "You'd do that for me? Go back to the lake, even with your father there?"

"I said I would, didn't I?"

"Yes, you surely did."

"Okay, then it's settled. If I can arrange things, we'll go Saturday morning."

"Okay." She still looked as if she didn't quite believe him, and he didn't believe he'd just agreed to go back to the one place on earth he didn't want to see again.

Wanting to gain her trust, Mason tried to sound cheerful. "It'll be good to see your family, especially your father. We both know how he just adores his new son-in-law."

That made her grin. "He might take you fishing for Old Man."

"Old Man? Don't tell me your father has captured one of your former suitors and turned him into a swamp creature."

"No, Old Man is the biggest bass on Caddo Lake, according to my daddy and the twins. They've been after him for years now."

"Oh, so if I go and I happen to catch Old Man, I'd better throw him back for your father, right?"

"That would be wise."

They laughed then, cutting the tension and awareness that had been floating around them like an invisible wind.

"Want to see the finished product before our guests arrive?" Lily asked, nervousness making her voice shaky.

"I like what I see so far," he commented as he touched a finger to her hair. "You did a good job."

His eyes were on her, not the newly decorated house. The way he looked at her made Lily feel as if she were indeed a delicate flower blossom floating on a dark swamp basin. Ah, but she knew that water lilies, no matter how delicate they looked, had roots that ran deep and held fast.

She'd just have to do the same.

"Well, c'mon," she said. "We don't have much time. The caterers are already in the kitchen and the clock is almost on seven."

"Lead the way, madam."

Although he'd seen the house as a work in progress, Lily wanted to see his reaction now that it was truly finished. She took him to the large formal living room, now filled with tasteful antiques and intriguing artwork, with everything from Remington sculptures to Georgia O'Keeffe prints gracing its spacious confines.

"It's amazing," Mason told her, his eyes scanning the room. "What did I have in here before, an armchair and a couch?"

"That's about it."

"I like the Georgia O'Keeffes. They make me think of you."

Lily beamed. "And the Remingtons made me think of you."

"The delicate mixed with the rugged, so to speak?"

She affected an air of superiority. "One might say that, might one?"

Mason couldn't help but laugh. Lily, being haughty, was almost as good as Lily being down-to-earth. Lifting his nose in the air, he replied on a nasal drawl, "Yes, one just might at that."

They moved on to the formal dining room across the hall. A long centuries-old mahogany table surrounded by twelve ornate chairs centered the room. Already the caterers had brought in silver trays of food, spreading it across the lacy white cloth covering the table and along the buffets and sideboards Lily and Pam had found to fill the big room.

"The furniture is exquisite and the food looks good," Mason said as he reached for a delicate canapé. Lily slapped his hand, but allowed him to sneak one more before she dragged him into the den that he used as his office and study.

Here she'd chosen leather, rich pine and oak woods, and braided rugs to give the modern room a cozy, Texas-style ambience.

"Ah, rawhide," Mason said, taking on an exaggerated drawl. "A manly room, ma'am. And a desk as big as Texas." Grinning, he rounded the heavy oak piece to settle back in the leather chair behind it. "And it sure beats that drab gray metal piece of junk I called an office." Gazing up at her, he tipped an imaginary hat. "At least you let me keep my computer. This ol' cowboy sure likes what you've done with the place."

"Well, this old cowboy might just fall off his horse when he gets the bill for all this rawhide," Lily told him, her hand trailing over the back of a rich tan-colored leather armchair.

He groaned then. "I guess that bill would be around here somewhere? By the way, where is everything anyway?"

Seeing his concerned frown as he searched for his precious paperwork, Lily nodded. "All of your files are intact. Pam helped me organize them just the way you like them." Then she walked to the far corner of the long room to turn on a lamp. "Did you see your armoire?"

Smiling proudly, she clasped her hands together. She'd kept this piece hidden until tonight. A surprise just for Mason.

Mason whistled low, then hurried over to the massive wooden structure taking center stage near the stone fireplace. "It's perfect, Lily. Even better than the one you insisted on putting in the guest room."

"And it has all of your necessary equipment," she quipped as she admired the rich, green-stained entertainment center. She didn't tell him that she'd personally stripped the wood and restained it herself. "Big screen for those Dallas Cowboy football games, and a stereo system for your listening pleasure, complete with remotes and other fancy gadgets. When you're not working at that big desk, you can plop down on the couch and play with your new toys."

"My own *Villa Finale*," Mason said, referring to a famous mansion in San Antonio. "It's…it's more than I expected, Lily."

From her? she wondered, then quickly told herself not to be so sensitive. "I'm glad you like it."

"I do." He turned on the stereo, testing. Music from the local public radio station filtered into the room, a classical tune that bespoke of waltzing in a summer garden.

"Dance with me," he said as he turned to face her.

Lily's heart lifted with each note of the Strauss waltz. Taking his hand, she followed him to the open space between the fireplace and the coffee table. There, they danced to the soft, soothing flow of violins, flutes and cellos.

"This is nice," Mason told her, his breath fanning her hair. "It will probably get crazy around here in about fifteen minutes. When it does, close your eyes, take a deep breath and remember this, okay?''

Lily leaned into him, savoring the strength, the security of his strong, sure arms, her newfound feelings of love pouring over her like a warm wind of hope. It could be like this always for them, if she could get past all of her insecurities and doubts. If she could get past her guilt.

Lifting her head, she looked up into Mason's eyes and saw the reflection of her own heart there. And it frightened her.

''I'd better get busy,'' she said, pulling away to straighten her hair. ''It's almost time.''

Mason watched as she hurried out of the room, her heels clicking on the wooden floor. Okay, so step two in his plan hadn't gone so well.

''Not almost time, Lily,'' he said as he switched off the music and listened to the silence of his newly decorated house. ''Way past time for us, darling. Way past time for us to be a real husband and wife.''

Step two—woo his wife with romance and charm, while he practiced patience and persistence.

''That'll be the hard one,'' he told himself as he headed toward the kitchen.

Luckily he already had several wooing techniques moving into action. Beginning tonight.

Wouldn't she be in for a surprise?

An hour later, Lily stood by her husband's side, greeting people as they moved through the house.

Her smile, as genuine as it was, seemed plastered in place, and somewhere near her right temple, a nasty headache was announcing its plans to get worse. But overall, she was pleased. The party was a success.

"They love you," Mason said close to her ear, as if reading the doubt in her eyes. "I told you you didn't have any reason to be worried."

"I wasn't so much worried about all of them," she replied, but another round of handshakes and well wishes caused him to turn away before she could explain. Which was just as well. How could she tell him that she wanted to please him, that she wanted to make him proud? How could she tell him that she felt so out of place, here amid the Dallas elite?

And yet she smiled. The food was great, the music soft and unintrusive, and most of the guests seemed warm and friendly, if not a bit pretentious.

But not everyone. Pam and Robert had been a great comfort and help. Even now they were circulating, making sure everyone was being taken care of and pampered. Lily watched them, longing for the easy companionship they shared. When would things change between Mason and her? They had such rare moments, such as when he'd danced with her earlier, and then *poof,* everything went back to business as usual. She wasn't sure she could continue to deceive herself and everyone else. It wasn't right.

The minister from the neighborhood church

walked up to greet them then, a sure sign that Lily needed to stay focused on entertaining her guests, instead of drifting in a sea of self-pity.

"Reverend O'Neil," she said, relieved to see someone she knew to be sincere. "I'm so glad you came."

"Me, too," the plump, red-haired preacher said. "That Tex-Mex buffet had me going back for seconds."

Mason laughed and shook his hand. "We've got an Italian buffet out near the pool."

"Oh, I'm in real trouble," the preacher replied, patting his girth. "I'm supposed to be on that new-fangled diet everyone's talking about—the one where you aren't allowed to enjoy food so much."

"Not tonight," Lily said, glad that the minister and his wife were having a good time. "I don't want any leftovers."

"No fear of that," Reverend O'Neil replied. "And I haven't even sampled the dessert table yet."

"There you are." His wife, Suzi, found her husband and gave him a gentle pat on the back. "Did I hear you mention dessert?"

"I can't deny it," Reverend O'Neil said, his admission sheepish. "We were talking about that very thing."

"I think you can have one nibble," Suzi replied, her green eyes sparkling. "We'll just have to walk an extra mile tomorrow morning."

"She is a tough taskmaster," the preacher said as

he followed his slender wife to the coffee and desserts nestled on a sideboard.

Turning to Mason, Lily noticed he was once again checking his watch. He'd been glancing at it over and over for the past half hour. "What is the matter with you?" she asked, worried that he was bored.

"Nothing," Mason replied, his eyes scanning the crowd. "I...I was just expecting someone."

The front door opened then and he smiled. Lily's concern turned to relief as she watched his face. "Well, whoever it is—"

The words died on her lips as her gaze followed his. There at the door stood her parents and the twins, all dressed to the nines, and looking as lost as four wood ducks in the middle of a lake full of swans.

Mason's smile turned into a full-fledged, completely smug expression of delight. "Ah, there they are. I was getting worried."

"Mason?" Lily couldn't believe her family was standing here in the hallway of her new home. "You invited my folks?"

"Yes. You don't mind, do you?"

"Of course not," she said as he guided her to them. She hadn't realized until this minute how much she missed her family.

"Oh, Lily," Cora said when she spied them coming across the hallway. "I almost didn't recognize you. You look so lovely."

Bill Norton, wincing and huffing against the only

tie he owned, a lovable old thing with a horrible fish motif that brought tears of joy to Lily's eyes, replied, "Well, who would? She's changed. A lot."

Jeremy and Pete stood there in their Sunday best, their adolescent eyes taking in the crowd, the food and the luxury of their sister's new life. Lily saw their minds working before their mouths even started moving.

"Boy, oh, boy. Brother, we've certainly hit pay dirt now," Jeremy said under his breath.

"Yessir, ol' Lil did okay for herself," his brother agreed.

Both met the wrath of their father's unyielding eyes. "What did I tell both of you not ten minutes ago, before we even got out of the van?"

Pete looked down at his spiffy loafers, then squinted. "To behave, keep our opinions to ourselves and...don't embarrass our sister?"

"That's it, exactly," Cora said, taking charge as she pushed her husband toward Lily and Mason. "You both look so...happy." She hugged them close, one arm around each of them, forcing them way too close together for Lily's comfort.

"We are," Mason told her, his eyes briefly settling on Lily. "We're happy you could make it. And as I told you on the phone, you're welcome to stay all weekend."

"But—" Lily glanced from her hopeful, happy family to the supposedly happy man at her side. So he'd invited her family here just to avoid going back to the lake? He must have called them right after he'd agreed to the trip, just over two hours ago. Oh, the nerve of him. And so like Mason to make a decision without telling her or allowing her the courtesy of discussing it first. So like her husband to take matters into his own hands, to be able to control things in his own way.

But she couldn't very well make a scene right here, right now, with all his friends and her own family watching. And he knew it.

"But of course, we'd love to have you stay," she said, her sharp gaze hitting on her husband before she saw her father giving her a look of concern.

"We wouldn't be putting you out, would we, honey? 'Cause we sure don't have to stay." Bill glared at Mason, indicating he'd like nothing better than to take the lot of them, including his daughter, home.

"No, no." Lily rushed to hug her father close. "I'm so glad to see you. Mason likes to surprise me and he certainly did. But…it was very kind of him to do this." Lifting her face away from her father's sweet cheek, she said, "Please, Daddy, stay. I want you to see what I've done with the house."

"Okay," Bill said, relief clear on his ruddy features. "Oh, I almost forgot." He looked over at Mason now. "I've got a surprise of my own. Mason, your daddy's outside. He didn't want to come, but we insisted. Thought we might as well make this a real family affair."

It was Mason's turn to look shocked.

Lily couldn't help but feel sorry for him. His stubborn way of controlling the situation had just backfired on him.

Very badly.

And she had a feeling that the entire weekend was about to end up that way, too.

Chapter Eleven

"But Lily, I had already invited them. I didn't want to spoil the surprise."

Mason realized way too late that Lily didn't really like surprises. And he had another one coming, tonight.

His carefully orchestrated ideas just weren't going according to plan at all.

"But you should have told me," she said as she stood in the middle of the upstairs sitting room. "I would have been more prepared. The guest rooms need fresh linens."

"I'll help you make the beds," Mason told her, coming to stand in front of her, one hand on each of her arms. "I didn't mean to upset you. Honestly."

Lily wanted to believe him, needed to see that he really had been trying to do something sweet and considerate for her. "So you'd already invited them? You didn't call them tonight, after we agreed to go to the lake?"

"No, of course not." Throwing up his hands, he said, "They couldn't have dressed, packed and been over here so quickly if I'd called them tonight, right?"

He had a point there. Even with her mother's brilliant organization, it always took her dad and the twins several trips back to the house, before they could ever load up and go anywhere. Not to mention, going by to pick up Curtis, too.

"Okay," she said at last. "You did a good and noble thing. Thank you."

"You don't sound so pleased," Mason replied. "Aren't you glad to see them?"

"Of course I am," she told him as she went about straightening the already immaculate room, one hand rubbing the throbbing ache in her temple. "We'll put Mom and Dad in the big room downstairs. That way they'll have a little more privacy and their own bathroom. And the boys, they can take the room down the hall from me. That just leaves your father."

"Yes," Mason said, his expression somewhere between tired and drained. "What do we do about my father?"

Lily gave him a sympathetic look. "You certainly didn't plan on him being here, did you?"

Mason shrugged. "The best-laid plans—"

"I'm glad he came," Lily interjected. "And I'm proud of you for being civil about the whole thing. We'll have a nice visit."

"Oh, great. Not only do I have your father to contend with, but now I have mine, also. This was supposed to be a surprise for you, not a weekend of torture for me."

"Well, we can't send the man away. And since the bed we ordered for the other upstairs bedroom isn't here yet, the only room left is the one I've been staying in."

That brought his head up. Suddenly Mason understood why she was so bothered by all of this. She didn't know how to explain their platonic sleeping arrangements to their many houseguests. "I didn't think ahead to bunk assignments. I'm sorry."

"Well, I'm thinking about it now," she retorted. "And that means some new arrangements."

With a businessman's shrewd calculation, Mason saw the significance of the problem, as well as the benefits of the solution. "You're going to put him in your room?"

"Unless you want him to stay with you?"

"No." His eyes held hers, while his heart held out hope. "So, Mrs. Winslow, does this mean you're officially moving across the hall?"

Lily wanted to tell him, that officially, she was ready to be his wife in every sense of the word. But not tonight, not when her emotions were in turmoil and her mind was whirling. "We don't have any other choice," she pointed out with what she hoped was a practical application. "I don't want to have to explain—"

"Why we don't share a room," Mason finished for her. "Okay, you can take the bed and I'll sleep on the couch by the fireplace. It's comfortable enough."

"I can sleep on the couch," Lily replied, her heart dropping. He didn't want her there. She was sure of it.

"No, I won't let you do that. I'll be fine on the couch. If I can't sleep, I'll just enjoy watching you."

That remark, so intimate, so sincere, caught Lily completely off guard. To hide the sweet sensations cresting like storm waves in her stomach, she nodded. "All right. We'll argue logistics later. Right now we need to get back downstairs. It's getting late and we have to say goodbye to our guests."

"And...see what else the evening will bring," Mason said, almost to himself.

"Let's hope no more surprises," Lily teased, her smile full of forgiveness. "Mason?"

"Hmmm?"

"You are a very thoughtful man."

With that she gave him a chaste kiss on the cheek and left him standing in the middle of the small room with the big fan-light window. Turning to that window, Mason looked out over the moonlit summer night. "I hope you still think that when the new car arrives," he said.

* * *

After Lily had hurriedly moved some of her most obvious possessions over to Mason's room, she started back downstairs to find her parents. They had taken an immediate liking to Reverend O'Neil, so they were out by the pool, talking to him and Suzi. And she had suggested that the twins might want to check out Mason's entertainment system. So she knew exactly where her brothers were. But where was Curtis Winslow?

After learning that his father was here, Mason had gone out the front door to at least bring the man inside. Knowing how much that had cost him, Lily was proud of him. It was a first step, although a rather awkward one.

Curtis had entered the house like a man sentenced to execution, barely nodding to her or anyone else. Luckily Cora had handled the situation in her usual assured fashion. "We're starved. How about trying one of those buffets?"

Then Lily had teamed them up with Reverend O'Neil, who knew some of the background, and he'd blessedly taken matters from there. But Curtis had hung back, silent and sullen, his expression a mixture of pain and pride.

Deciding she'd better check on him, Lily now began a search of all the downstairs rooms. She was making her way through the kitchen toward the open patio doors when voices from the nearby powder room caught her attention.

"She's not what I expected," came a shrill admonishment.

This was followed by, "No, kind of homely, don't you think? And Mr. Winslow is such a hunk. I always thought—"

"Thought what? That he could do better than some backwoods widow woman? Maybe you thought he'd fall head over heels in love with you?"

"Well, at least I have the right hairstyle. Can you believe that prim bun? And that dress—very plain."

"She's country. They dress that way in the country."

Lily stood still, her hand to her mouth. They were actually talking about *her*. Self-consciously, she ran a hand through her upswept hair, then turned to leave before the two women emerged from the powder room.

But it was too late. She pivoted to find Curtis Winslow standing there, and from the look on his face, he'd heard every word, too.

Then, to make matters worse, the women came out, giggling and whispering, only to stop and stare with openmouthed embarrassment at the source of their gossip.

"Mrs. Winslow!"

Lily recognized the young girls. They both worked for Mason. One was from the accounting department and one worked directly under Pam as a clerical assistant.

"Hello, ladies," Lily said, her head high, her

smile serene, in spite of the hurt inside her heart. "Are you enjoying the party?"

"Yes, ma'am," the tall blonde named Kaye said. "Everything...everything is just great."

"Yeah, great," her brunette friend, Patty, added, bobbing her head like a lure on a hook. "We...we were just getting ready to leave though."

Lily's smile stayed in place as she waited for the embarrassed women to pass, but Curtis's face was the same deep red as Kaye's short dress.

"You two," he said, reaching up a shaky hand to halt the suddenly quiet duo. "I heard someone introducing you to Lily's parents outside. Don't you both work for my son?"

Kaye nodded, her eyes going wide. "Yes, sir."

Curtis nodded right back, then leaned against the tiled counter at his back. "Bet Mason wouldn't like it one bit if he knew two of his employees were saying things about his wife behind her back—"

"Curtis, it's all right," Lily interrupted, her look imploring. She wouldn't give these two the satisfaction of any kind of defense. It would only make matters worse if she threatened them or reprimanded them.

"No, it's not all right," Curtis said, waving a bony hand in the air. "You girls don't know this here woman. I myself only just met her a few weeks ago, but she took up for me, and gave me a place to stay. And she calls me on a regular basis to see how I'm holding up. So that makes her okay in my book, you understand?''

The brunette lowered her head. ''We didn't mean—''

''I know exactly what you meant,'' Curtis told the repentant woman. ''And I think you both owe my daughter-in-law an apology.''

''That's not necessary,'' Lily said quietly.

''Yes, it is,'' Curtis replied even more quietly.

''I'm sorry,'' Kaye said, her eyes lifting to meet Lily's. ''We were way out of line.''

''Yes,'' her friend agreed. ''We…we were just being mean and inconsiderate. You won't tell Mr. Winslow, will you?''

''Worried about your jobs, huh?'' Curtis said, a chuckle emitting from his skinny frame.

Lily held up a hand then. ''I don't think my husband would fire anyone over their opinions. He's not that kind of man.''

Curtis nodded. ''Yeah, but I'm just the kind of man who'd be glad to tell him what happened here tonight. So, ladies, my advice to you is to take this as a lesson. And be glad that Mrs. Winslow is a gracious, understanding lady.''

Both women nodded and bobbed their heads in unison, then hurried to leave, their heads down, their faces drained of all color by the tongue-lashing they'd just received.

Lily watched them go, then turned to Curtis.

"Thank you. I appreciate the vote of confidence and the kind words."

"I meant it," he said, and then he ambled back out into the night, a loner in the middle of the crowd.

Lily took a deep breath, then stepped inside the powder room to regain her composure. Spying her reflection in the mirror, she couldn't help but remember the biting words of the women Curtis had just dressed down.

Were they right about her? Her hair *was* plain, her dress *was* simple, and…she was miserable. Maybe it was time for that makeover she'd promised herself. She would never want to embarrass Mason in any way. Especially with her country ways and her homely looks. She'd just have to work on fixing both.

Closing her eyes, she felt a fierce pride for Curtis Winslow, though. He reminded her so much of Daniel, standing there, firm in his opinion. And he reminded her of Mason, too. Stepping in to do battle, taking charge to set things right. Those Winslow men…they were all very special in her book.

Now she was glad she'd kept in touch with Mason's father. Not because she needed someone in her corner, but because he obviously longed to have someone in his.

I won't turn my back on him, Lord, she silently pledged. No matter how much Mason disliked the man.

Lily came out of the bathroom to find Pam, looking sophisticated and glamorous in a glittering gold cocktail dress, refilling her glass of punch from the bowl on the counter.

"Lily, there you are. I've been looking for you. How are you?"

"I've been better."

Instantly Pam was at her side. "What's wrong?"

"I have a splitting headache and I'm exhausted."

Pam gave her a knowing look. "And now you have houseguests for the weekend."

"Courtesy of my very thoughtful husband."

Pam laughed, then whispered. "He had all the right intentions."

"I know. And I'm glad to see them here, really."

"But…?"

Lily shrugged. "But…it's all these other people. I'm just not sure I'm cut out to be the wife of such an important man."

"You're doing fine," Pam assured her. "And you know Mason adores you, right?"

Because of the headache and the conversation she'd just overheard, it hurt to smile, but Lily made the effort anyway. "Of course he does."

Pam put an arm around her shoulder. "Which is exactly why he sent me to look for you. Mason has something he wants to give you."

"Oh, boy. Another surprise."

"That's our Mason. Always thinking ahead."

Lily wondered what he'd cooked up this time. "How can he possibly top what he's already done?"

"Oh, you'll just have to see for yourself," Pam told her as she herded Lily toward the front of the house.

He topped it all right, Lily thought a few minutes later. This time he'd gone completely over the top.

Pam ushered Lily out the front door, where the crowd of remaining guests stood gathered on the circular driveway. And in the middle, stood her husband, beaming a shaky smile that told her he wasn't so sure this was a good idea, after all.

But there he stood, trying to save face, in front of a brand-new bright red sports car. A big white ribbon was wrapped across the black convertible top, the word *Lily* sprayed across it with looping gold-colored letters.

"What's this?" Lily asked, her mouth dropping open.

"It's a car," Jeremy piped up, his hand moving over the bright red curve of the sleek vehicle. "And I do mean *car*."

Bill Norton grabbed his son and tugged him away from the object of his desire. "Hush up."

Pete had the good sense to stay away, but his eyes were just as bright as his brother's. "Well, get in, Lily. Test it out."

Lily glanced at her excited sibling, then spied her embarrassed husband. "Mason, I thought we were going to go car shopping together."

"We were…uh, but…well, you were so busy with the house. I just thought—"

Bill Norton snorted, obviously thrilled to see his son-in-law groping for words. "You thought wrong, son," he said, his expression grim. "Lily won't drive that thing."

"You will, won't you, Lily?" Pete asked, hope in each word. "At least take us for a spin."

"Can't fit both of us in there," his brother pointed out, grinning. "I'll be glad to take the first test drive with her, though."

He was headed around the car, intent on getting in the passenger's side, when his father once again grabbed him by the collar. "You'll do no such thing. This vehicle is way too dangerous for you, even if you're not driving."

"Well, can we—drive it, that is?" Pete asked his sister.

"No" came the answer, in unison, from his parents.

Pete hung his head, then lifted his eyes to Lily. "Are you gonna keep it?"

"No," Lily said finally, her gaze on her husband. "Mason, this was really a nice gesture on your part, but…I kinda wanted a truck."

"A truck!" Jeremy groaned and whirled around in a circle of disbelief. "The man buys you a Porsche and you tell him you'd rather have a truck. I don't understand—"

His father's hand none-too-gentle on his arm stopped him from saying anything further.

"I need a truck," Lily explained, hoping she could make Mason see, "because I like to haul stuff. And I intend on doing lots of landscaping. I'll be hauling dirt, bedding plants, fertilizer."

"Not in that," Pete told her redundantly and reluctantly.

"Exactly," Lily replied, throwing up her hands. "It's beautiful, Mason. But not very practical."

Mason sighed long and hard, ran a hand through his hair, then looked down at the beautiful machine he'd had specially ordered from his friend Ray at the foreign car place in Dallas. On a voice edged with impatience, he tried to patiently explain his actions. "Of course it's not practical. It's a gift. A fun gift—something to enjoy and have a good time with."

"I don't need a good time, I need a truck," Lily told him, her hands on her hips. Then, glancing around to see the curious eyes following her every word, she added, "But we can discuss this later. It's a beautiful car, Mason."

With that, she walked over to him and kissed him on the cheek. "Thank you. You're just full of surprises tonight." Then she whispered for his ears only, "And please tell me this is the last one."

"It is," he said, hugging her close for a second. "I'm sorry. I messed up again, didn't I?"

"In the best possible way," Lily told him with a smile of condolence.

He let her go, then looked down at her. "So you want a truck?"

"That's what she said," Bill offered. "That's my Lily—practical and smart. Too smart for the likes of some." He gave his son-in-law a pointed look.

Jeremy, apparently heartbroken, added, "Well, with what this machine cost, you can probably buy two trucks, with double caps and mud-eating tires."

Lily laughed then, breaking the tension. "No, I'll buy a sensible economy-size truck with a good, solid flatbed and an air conditioner and radio, at least."

Pete eyed her curiously. "Are we really related?"

"I'm afraid so," his sister told him, ruffling his spiked hair. "Sorry, boys. I know you're both drooling over this car, but it goes back, first thing tomorrow."

"Can we at least take a spin?" Jeremy asked on a whine.

Lily looked toward her father. "What do you think?"

Bill looked formidable for a minute, then said, "I guess one spin around the block wouldn't hurt. You driving?"

"Why don't you?" Lily asked, smiling as her dad's eyes lit up. "Just don't speed, okay?"

"Okay." Bill hurried to the driver's seat, then motioned for his sons. The boys were already arguing over who got to ride first.

"Alphabetically," Bill said, telling Jeremy to get in. "Petey, you can have the next turn."

"If you two ever come back," Cora hollered after them.

"I'll drive Pete, if you don't feel up to it," Mason offered.

Reverend O'Neil spoke up. "I was kinda hoping I could take her for a spin myself."

"Men and their machines," Cora stated, rolling her eyes. Mrs. O'Neil nodded her agreement.

"That's fine," Lily replied, laughing as she took her husband's arm.

The next few minutes went by as fast as the car, which made frequents trips around and around the long driveway until most of the remaining men in the crowd had had their "turn."

Soon, all of the guests had left and Lily was alone with her family and her husband. Looking around the house, she noted that the caterers had done a great job of cleaning up. Not much left to do but go to bed.

Then she remembered where she'd be sleeping tonight.

Well, she'd just use this time alone with Mason to set a few ground rules about this marriage, and about surprises. Since she probably wouldn't get much sleep, at least she could get a few things straight with her new husband.

Chapter Twelve

❧

Mason came out of the bathroom to find Lily pacing in front of the still, empty fireplace, her cotton robe drawn up to her neck, her dark hair loose and flowing down her back.

He stopped to lean into the door frame. How many times had he envisioned her here with him, just like this? How many times had he longed to go across the hall, lift her into his arms and bring her back inside this room where she truly belonged?

Now that she was here, he wasn't quite sure what to do about her. He knew what he wanted, but he also knew Lily wasn't ready. He could see it in her very being, in her nervous pacing, in the way she averted her eyes away from him.

"I don't bite," he said on a defeated note. "You can look at me, at least."

"I'm sorry," Lily said as she whirled around. "All ready for bed?"

"Yes," he replied, thinking sleep was the furthest thing from his mind. "I am beat. Remind me next time I want to have a party, invite surprise guests for the weekend and give you a fabulous gift, that doing all of those things in one night can take its toll on a man."

She looked up then, her smile breaking through like a ray of sunlight lifting over dark waters. "You are something else, do you know that?"

"I think I do, but please don't tell me what that something else might be." Lifting away from the door, he added, "I'm sorry, Lily. About the surprise guests, about the car, about everything."

About us? she wanted to ask, remembering the hurtful words she'd heard earlier from the two young women in the powder room. Instead she just stared across the big room at him, thinking he looked even better in his pajamas than he did in a tuxedo. Wanting to offer him some sort of comfort, she said, "Mason, you didn't do anything so wrong. I'm glad my parents and the twins are here, and I'm especially glad your father came with them."

"But?"

"No buts, really. Okay, there is one but."

"What?"

"I'd appreciate it if you'd stop doing these things without at least talking to me first. And I don't just mean that fancy car parked out in the driveway."

She lifted her shoulders in a shrug. "You practically planned tonight's party without consulting me, then told me what you expected—"

"I gave you total control over that," he interjected in his own defense.

"Yes, after I pointed out a few things," she reminded him.

"Which just goes to show I can change," he countered. "I want to change. I want us to—"

He stopped, at a loss for words. How could he tell her that he wanted to be the best husband to her, the best husband in all ways. How could he spend the night in this room with her, without declaring his love to her? But that might turn her away just as badly as the new sports car had. He was too flashy, too pushy and too materialistic for Lily's tastes. If Lily realized he'd always loved her, she'd probably be disgusted with him, think he lured her into this marriage too quickly because of his own controlling needs.

"*I* want us to come to an understanding," she said, finishing the sentence he couldn't. "First, no more big surprises. I can handle the little ones, like when you gave me my ring." She looked into his eyes, her smile warming his heart. "That was a surprise—classic Mason. But my ring—" she looked down at the shining diamond nestled on her finger "—now, this ring is perfect. Not too gaudy, not too brash…just right. And even though you did embarrass me to no end, proposing like that right in front of my folks, it's as if you knew what I'd like, exactly which kind of ring I'd pick myself. And this is that ring. This ring says it all.''

Mason stood there, the lump in his throat warring with the ache in his heart as he fell for her all over again. What he saw there in her eyes as she gazed at that ring—that was what he wanted to see in her eyes each time she gazed at him. Well, if he'd hit it right once, he was sure he could do it again. He could win her love, one step at a time.

Immediately he agreed to her stipulations. "Okay, only small surprises. I can do that."

Lily grinned. "And you'll take the car back?"

"Yes, I guess. But your dad will be heartbroken."

"He did take a liking to it," she said, shaking her head as she chuckled. "Even though he'd never admit it."

"Just like his daughter."

"Oh, I love the car. But I—"

He held up a hand. "I know, you need a truck." Then it was his turn to shake his head in wonder. "Lily, you are truly unique. Most women would kill for a Porsche."

"I'll settle for a Chevy," she replied. "And I can't wait to get this yard in order. I'm just sorry we ran out of time before the party."

"Speaking of the party, did you have a good time?"

She hesitated, then shrugged. "It was lovely. Everything was so nice. Those caterers Pam hired sure knew their stuff. I hardly had to lift a finger.''

Mason watched as she lowered her eyes, her head down. She seemed so distant, so resigned. Of course, being here with him like this would make her feel that way. He had to wonder, though, if there was something else bothering her. Had she really enjoyed being with all his high-powered friends and most of his employees? Did she resent all the caterers and decorators, telling her how to run her own house? Lily was used to doing things her way, after all. And he needed to take that into consideration.

"About the yard…" he began, hoping to make her feel better. "If you don't want a team of landscapers roaming around, just do whatever you'd like. I don't want you to work too hard by yourself, but you're the boss."

"No, we're in this together," she told him as she came around the couch. "Which brings me to the other thing I wanted to discuss with you."

"Oh, and what's that?"

"I want your father to stay here with us a while."

Mason stared at her as if he hadn't heard her right. "What did you say?"

"I think Curtis should stay here this week, and we can take him home next weekend."

Mason shook his head. "No. Lily, I can agree to less control, less surprises, less anything, but I won't agree to my father staying here."

"And why not?"

"You know why not."

"No, I don't. Not really. I only know that you're bitter and indifferent and…he's getting old, Mason. He needs to reconcile things with his son."

Mason stomped over to the window, holding back the anger that threatened to make him lose control. "Well, you're right about one thing—I am bitter and I don't care about his guilt or his need to make things better. The man ran out on us, Lily. And until you've lived through something such as that, you have no idea how it makes a person feel inside."

Lily came to him then, touching a hand to his arm. "I think I have a pretty good idea how being abandoned can make a person feel, Mason. I can see that by the way you're acting." Willing him to turn to her, she looked up into his eyes. "Let me help you. Let me be the peacemaker between you and your father."

"No," he said, pushing her away as he stormed past her so she wouldn't see the pain in his eyes. "No. Just stay out of this, Lily."

"I can't." She tried to explain. "I saw how your father's leaving caused Daniel to be the way he was. And now I can see how it's affected you, too. We can't make this a true marriage, a real partnership until you settle things with your father."

He faced her, his expression grim. "No, this won't be a true marriage as long as you keep forcing me to be around that man," Mason shouted, his eyes blazing. And because he was hurt and lost, he added,

"And not as long as I'm sleeping on the couch and you're sleeping in the bed."

"So much for changing," Lily replied, her own anger justifying the statement.

Within minutes, they'd turned out the lights, silent there in the darkness, shrouded in moonlight, mad at each other. Lily lay in the big bed, so very aware of her husband sleeping on the long couch across the room. Unable to stop herself, she reached out a hand to touch the pillow on the other side of the bed. It felt cold and bare, just like her soul was feeling right now.

She had no way of knowing Mason clutched his own pillow and thought about her. She had no way of knowing that his heart was breaking as he listened to her breathing and wished he could carry the sound peacefully into his dreams.

But Mason could find no peace tonight. Not with Lily just a few feet away, yet so far out of his reach. And not with his father sleeping across the hall, just as Mason had longed for him to do all those years ago. But he refused to reach out to his father; he refused to give up or give in.

So he lay there in the dark and held fast to his hardened heart, his eyes wide open.

Mason went to work early the next morning, on the excuse that he had some paperwork to finish up before he could officially begin his weekend. That left Lily to entertain her perplexed relatives.

"Everything okay, honey?" Cora asked after they cleared the breakfast table. "You look tired."

"I guess I am tired," Lily confessed. "I didn't sleep very well." Looking out the window, she watched as her father and the twins roughhoused in the chilly pool waters, while Curtis sat in the shade of the patio table's broad umbrella, content to watch from the sidelines. "I'm still adjusting to all of this, I suppose."

Cora looked around the elaborate kitchen. "Yep, this house is sure different from the lake house. Do you feel out of place here?"

Lily turned to face her mother. Cora could always sense when something wasn't right with her only daughter. "Yes," she said finally. "I don't know *my* place here yet, Mama. And last night, I heard these two girls who work for Mason, talking about how plain I am, how *country*."

Cora came to her and patted her shoulder. "Now you're not going to let idle talk discourage you, are you, daughter?"

"I'm trying not to let what they said get to me," Lily replied. "But…what if I don't live up to my part of this deal? What if I disappoint Mason?"

"Has he given you reason to think you disappoint him?" Cora asked, her gaze full of understanding and worry.

"No, but—" Lily stopped, thinking she couldn't tell even her mother the intimate details of her life here. "I don't know. He's so angry at his father, and he refuses to even talk to Curtis. I want Curtis to stay here with us for a few days, and Mason and I fought about it last night.''

Cora folded her arms across her waist, then glanced out the window. ''I see. So this is about more than just what some silly young girls said.''

''Yes, I guess it is.''

Cora straightened the colorful linen place mats on the breakfast table. ''Honey, I know you mean well, but you can't push Mason and his father together. That has to come from them. Both of them.''

''But I can't stand by and watch Mason like this. He's in so much pain and it's affecting our marriage. He's still angry because I let his father stay in the lake house, but I couldn't turn the man away from what used to be his home.''

''I know,'' Cora replied. ''And I believe you did the right thing. You know, we've spent a lot of time with Curtis and I can tell you this much—that man is hurting, too. I believe he came home to die, Lily.''

''I've thought that myself,'' Lily told her as she watched Mason's father out in the yard. ''He seems so frail, so weak. But I don't think Mason has even noticed.''

''Oh, he's noticed, all right,'' Cora said. ''And it's scaring him. He realizes he's going to lose his father all over again.''

Lily lifted her head. ''So that's why he refuses to get close to Curtis? He doesn't want to go through that again?''

"It makes sense," Cora replied. "First his mother, then Daniel. And his father left when he was so young. I don't think Mason is ready to face this reconciliation just yet, because he can't handle what might be down the road."

Lily sighed, then hugged her mother close. "Any suggestions?"

"Watch and pray," Cora quoted. "And you need to concentrate on your marriage." Cora stepped back, then touched a hand to Lily's cheek. "Make it work, Lily, with prayer and consideration. Take this gift and celebrate it each and every day. Show Mason that someone can love him, that he can learn to return love. He'll find solace with you and he'll find his way back to trusting God again, with your help."

Later that day, Lily remembered her mother's words and made a promise to God to be the best wife possible for Mason. He had suffered so much loss in his life, he had forgotten how to open up his heart to the possibilities of love. He needed her now more than ever, and she wanted to show him that she could be a good wife. She wouldn't pressure him about Curtis anymore. Instead she would just continue to get to know Curtis and show him that she cared about his well-being, while she worked on her marriage.

Starting today. She made an appointment to get her hair styled, and Cora agreed to go to the mall with her, to do some shopping for that much-needed wardrobe. They left the twins and Bill and Curtis watching a sports program on cable, while they headed out. Mason had managed to stay away most of the day, but had called to say he'd be back in time for dinner at least. And that would give Lily just enough time to transform herself into the kind of wife Mason expected her to be. It would be his turn to be surprised.

Mason got home earlier than he'd planned, and was surprised to find his house full of males and his television blasting a popular outdoors program.

"Hello, everyone," he said from the doorway of the den, his voice rising over the sound of Billy Clyde Bob somebody-or-other explaining the intricate mastery of fly-fishing on a whitewater river. Right now Mason wished he was faraway on some river, instead of standing here with his father's condemning eyes following him around the room.

"Oh, hey, Mase," Jeremy said, waving a hand without turning his head.

Pete grunted, then slapped a hand on his denim-clad leg. "Wow, I'd love to go there someday, catch some salmon." Then, "How ya doing, Mase?"

Mase nodded and grunted back. "My day clearly hasn't been as much fun as yours."

Bill spoke up then, his eyes centered on Mason like a hawk zooming in for its prey. "The ladies are out shopping at some fancy mall. Said they'd be back by five."

"The Galleria," Mason replied, happy that Lily had finally taken him up on going shopping for herself. "That's good. Lily needed a day away from here."

Curtis got up then to slowly walk over to his son. "Seems she needs more than just a day away."

Mason glared at his father, then turned to the snack bar located behind a counter. Grabbing a bottle of water out of the small refrigerator, he twisted the top off before responding. "And just what is that supposed to mean?"

Curtis looked to make sure Bill and the twins were still watching the television show. "She got her feelings hurt last night."

Mason went still, the bottle raised in midair. "What are you talking about?"

Curtis shuffled his feet, his head bent. "Two of your guests said some things…about Lily. She happened up on them and heard most of it. At about the same time, I came inside the house and I heard them, too. And I saw how she looked. She was embarrassed, but she was gracious, all the same."

"Who said these *things?*" Mason asked, fury moving like quicksand through his body. "And what exactly did they say?"

"I ain't saying who," Curtis replied, shaking his head. "I promised Lily I wouldn't. But they made fun of her, the way she was dressed, the way she wore her hair. Just jealous I think."

"Yes, just jealous," Mason said, swallowing

down half of the bottled water in one long gulp. "How could anyone be so cruel, and to Lily of all people?"

Curtis nodded. "I told them what kind a person she is, told them she'd done right by me—and I made them apologize. I don't think they'll be talking about her again anytime soon."

Mason studied his father's face, saw the sincerity there in the watery depths of his eyes. "I appreciate you doing that. Thank you."

"I did it for Lily," Curtis bluntly told him. "You're lucky to have that woman, son."

Mason couldn't deny that, even if it did rankle him, coming from this man. "Yes, I am." Then, in order to regain control over the strange emotions pushing at the door of his soul, he added, "And don't call me 'son.'"

Mason watched as Curtis took the intentional reprimand with a steady, measured look and head held high. "Look, I'm not out to gain points with you here. Just thought you might like to know, is all."

With that, he turned and shuffled back to the armchair in the corner, his back turned to Mason. When Mason glanced up, he saw Bill Norton watching him intensely.

Great. Now he had both of them on his back. But, he thought as he nodded amicably toward Lily's father, he was grateful to Curtis for coming to Lily's defense. Maybe his father had stood by her because Lily had come to Curtis's defense when no one else had been willing to step forward. Including his own son.

Mason stared at his father now, noticing again how skinny Curtis Winslow was, how measured each breath he took seemed to be, how frail his father looked, sitting in the big armchair. And he had to wonder—where had Curtis been all this time, what had he seen and done out there away from his family? And why was he back?

No, Mason told himself as he finished his water, then tugged at his necktie. *I won't be curious about him. I refuse to care, one way or the other, about him or what he's done. And I won't care when he's gone again.*

Curtis looked up then, before Mason could turn away. His gaze caught his son's. They stared each other down, each silently asking the questions that neither was ready to hear, each defiant and stubborn in not giving any answers just yet, while the sounds of laughter and camaraderie between Bill Norton and his own sons contrasted sharply with the cold indifference between Mason and his father.

And then Mason heard another sound, the sound of his wife's laughter as the kitchen door opened and closed. Dropping his gaze away from his father, he breathed a sigh of relief. He'd been unreasonable last night, downright mean. And all day he'd pouted and pawed and wondered if he'd ever get it right with the woman he loved. He just wanted to see her face, to see her shining dark hair, to give her a smile and a silent apology. He just wanted to be in the same room with Lily. That would make him feel a whole lot better about things.

And then she walked in and all his apologetic thoughts went flying out in the air much like the fancy fishing lines being touted on the wide-screen television across the room.

"Lily," he said without thinking, as he stared across at his wife. "What on earth did you do to your hair?"

Chapter Thirteen

Lily dropped the shopping bags she'd been carrying, her gaze flying to Mason's stunned face. "I—I had it cut and styled," she said, her voice shaky, her eyes wide as she reached up to tug at the pouf of bangs and layers surrounding her head.

Jeremy glanced at his brother, then said in a reassuring way, "It'll grow back. Eventually."

Bill immediately thumped his son on the ear, then turned to his daughter, a what-on-earth look of confusion plastered on his ruddy face. "It looks…nice, honey. Really."

Pete, for once, remained completely silent, as he watched Mason with wide-eyed fascination.

Then, because Lily couldn't take the way they were all looking at her as if she'd sprouted antlers, she said, "Excuse me. I'll be upstairs if anyone needs me." Then she burst into tears and ran out of the room.

"Good going," Bill told Mason with a stern glare. "You hurt her feelings," he added with understated fury.

Mason groaned then ran a hand through his own hair. "Well, it was…just such a shock." Turning to Cora, he said, "Where's her hair?"

"Back at that fancy salon," Cora told him as she gathered up Lily's scattered packages to set them out of the way. "She wanted to look pretty, for you."

"I liked her the way she was," Mason told the entire room.

"Then go tell her that," Cora urged gently.

Mason took her advice, taking the stairs two at a time, only to find Lily in their bathroom, frantically combing all the tease out of her now chin-length, layered hair.

And she was still crying. Sobbing was more like it.

"Oh, Lily," he said as he stepped into the bathroom. "Honey, I'm sorry. It's…it's not a bad haircut."

"Yes it is," she told him through her tears. "I wanted something modern and easy to care for, and that…that man told me this was the latest style, very cutting edge." She wailed and threw her comb down. "He just didn't tell me he was going to chop my hair into shreds, then puff it up like a blowfish."

In spite of the crisis situation, Mason had to smile. It was a mistake.

"And now you're laughing at me," Lily said, her reflection catching his in the mirror. Lowering her head, she started crying all over again, then whirled to try to move past him.

Mason grabbed her, gently pulling her into his arms, his hands automatically going up to touch her hair. "Lily, listen to me, please." When she stilled in his arms, he kissed the layered fluff around her face, then lifted her chin with his thumb. "You are a beautiful woman. And I loved your hair just the way it was. I hope you didn't go and do this just because of what someone said last night."

At her look of shock, he added, "Curtis told me, but he wouldn't tell me who upset you. Is that what this is about?"

Lily sniffed, then shook her head. "Not really. I mean what those two said did bother me, but I know they're just young and immature and they didn't mean to be cruel. I can handle that kind of talk, Mason." Then her eyes welled with tears again. "I just can't handle being a big disappointment to you." She shrugged, then dropped her shoulders in defeat. "This house, this life-style—I just don't know if I'll ever fit in here. I don't know what you expect from me. I mean, I can't give you children, I don't have a job, or anything to call my own. I'm all done with decorating the house, so what's left?

Digging in the yards? I'm not a real wife, not like I should be. What am I here for, Mason?"

Mason held her there, his heart turning to shreds. He wanted to tell her that he loved her. He wanted to tell her that she was here because he needed her, because his brother had seen that need and acknowledged it with his blessings, but he couldn't bring himself to do that. What if she didn't believe him? Or worse, what if she didn't feel the same way?

Instead he grabbed her face between his hands and kissed her with a gentle branding. "You're here for this," he told her. "You're my wife now, Lily. And I think it's time we took this relationship one step further."

Lily looked so afraid, so unsure, he immediately wanted to take that suggestion back. But before he could, she surprised him with her next words.

"I've felt so bad, about our fight, about forcing you to reconcile with your father. I shouldn't have insisted—"

"You didn't do anything so wrong, Lily. And I'm not mad about that anymore. In fact, I spent all day thinking about what you said."

"You did?"

"Yes. You made some very valid points. Maybe I need to reconsider my feelings toward Curtis."

"Are you sure? About your father, about us?"

Mason kissed her again. "Very sure. How about you?"

She placed her hands over his, then brought them

down away from her face. "But I didn't think...I wasn't sure if you wanted me to..."

"To be my wife, in every sense of the word?"

She could only nod, her teary eyes wide and questioning.

"I want to make this a real marriage, Lily," he told her, careful of how he worded that declaration. "I'm very sure."

"Here? Now?" she whispered, the trace of a smile etching her tear-streaked face.

Mason stood there, listening to the sounds of laughter and chatter coming from somewhere in the house. "Maybe not right now, but soon. Very soon. As soon as we get rid of all our company."

"Oh, Mason." Then she started crying all over again. "But what about this?" She held a hand to her head, as if she had a tremendous headache.

Mason touched a finger to a wayward silky strand. "This is just as beautiful as it ever was." Tilting his head, he smiled down at her, his finger twirling through her hair. "I think I'm beginning to like *this.*"

"You're just trying to be nice," she countered.

"No, it does bring out your eyes." He kissed her wet lashes. "Such pretty eyes, too."

She looked skeptical in spite of her sigh.

"And your lips." He touched on a sprig of dark hair curled near her mouth. "It does bring out the curve in your lovely lips."

Then he kissed her again. "Tonight," he told her,

his expression full of hope and promise. "We don't have to wait for them to leave. Our bedroom is very remote and private."

"Tonight," she replied, a full smile forming on her face at last. Then she turned back to the mirror and rolled her eyes. "Well, Jeremy was right, at least. It will grow out."

"Eventually," Mason said, his grin gentle and reassuring. And eventually he hoped she would grow to love him in the same way he now loved her.

"Do you think it's the new hairdo?" Lily heard Jeremy ask Pete later as they all sat out around the pool, eating Texas-size grilled T-bones, complete with baked potatoes and salad.

"What are you two talking about?" Lily asked, her eyebrows raised.

"About you," Jeremy explained. "About you and Mason. You two were fighting, and he made you cry. You never cry, and now..." He shrugged, then glanced at his brother.

Pete knew the drill. Lily smiled as he finished his brother's sentence. "And now, well, you've got goo-goo eyes for him again, and he keeps smiling at you like a lovesick puppy or something. I thought he hated your hair."

"We talked things over," Lily explained, amused that her brothers were so confused about the ways of marriage. "He apologized and I accepted his apology. And now he likes my hair."

"It does look better since you combed that rat nest out of it," Pete admitted. "Man, when you first walked in—"

His brother hit him upside the head. "We're happy if you're happy, sis."

"I'm happy," Lily told them, her gaze searching out her husband. Mason smiled over at her, then lifted his tea glass in a silent salute.

"Making up is always the fun part," Cora whispered in Lily's ear as the twins, thoroughly disgusted with all this mushy sentiment, pushed at each other until they were both in the deep end of the pool.

"I guess so," Lily replied, her eyes still on Mason.

An undercurrent of awareness buzzed around them with all the tenacity of the mosquitoes being kept at bay by the bug zapper. But unlike those pests, what she felt for Mason could no longer be denied. And she no longer wanted to deny it. In spite of her tremendous guilt, Lily had made a vow to love, honor and cherish Mason. She intended to do just that. Somehow she'd have to deal with the guilt she felt over not having loved Daniel enough. Somehow she'd have to ask God to guide her and give her a second chance.

As if reading her doubts, Mason got up and came over to her. "The food was great, ladies," he said as he dropped his empty paper plate in the nearby trash can. "Cora, I'm so glad you-all decided to spend the weekend with us."

"We've had fun," Cora told him, her smile warm. "Guess we'll head home after church tomorrow, though."

Mason nodded, then turned to where Bill and Curtis sat deep in a discussion about Texas Rangers baseball. "Everyone, could I have your attention," he said, surprising Lily and Cora. When Bill and Curtis stopped talking to look up, and the boys quieted in the pool to gawk at him, he cleared his throat and said, "Lily and I have enjoyed having you here." Then after a minute of awkward silence, he looked down at his father. "And Dad, you are welcome to stay through the week if you'd like. We could take you home next weekend."

Curtis, clearly shocked, sat there looking up at his son, his expression quizzical and hopeful. Then his gaze shifted from Mason to Lily. "Did you put him up to this?"

Lily didn't know how to answer. Giving Mason a look of gratitude, she said, "I—I suggested it, yes. But I know Mason wouldn't ask if he didn't really want you here, Curtis. Would you please stay?"

Curtis struggled to stand. "It's mighty nice of you both to offer, but I've been helping Bill here around the bait shop. I like the work and it's peaceful, not so demanding. I don't want to shirk my duties."

"Then you don't want to stay?" Mason asked, a tinge of regret and reprimand evident in his voice.

Bill interjected. "Curtis, we can do without you for a few days."

"And I could use some advice and help with the landscaping," Lily pointed out.

Curtis didn't seem to hear either one of them. Turning back to Mason, he asked, "And how do you feel about this?"

Mason looked uncomfortable, then said, "I—I'd like you to stay. I'll have to work, of course, but you'd be good company for Lily, and I'll see you every night."

"Maybe you could take him out to one of your construction sites, too," Lily suggested. "That is…if he feels up to it."

Curtis stood there with his skinny hands tucked into the pockets of his polyester trousers, his head down. Finally he cleared his throat and said, "I reckon I could live with that. I'll try not to be a bother."

"No bother," Mason said, his eyes on his wife.

Cora cleared the air with her light laughter. "Then I guess that's all settled. Now we can look forward to a weekend visit from you two when you bring Curtis home."

"Yes," Lily said. "It'll be good to see the lake again."

"Fish are biting," Bill told her as he got up to take another sample of Cora's apple pie. "Old Man's been teasing me for weeks now. I aim to catch that fish before summer's over."

"You'll never catch Old Man," Pete called from the side of the pool. "That fish is too crafty."

"Watch me," Bill told his son, a big grin rounding his tanned face.

They all laughed at that, but Lily couldn't take her eyes off her husband. Mason stood there with his heart in his hand, and she could tell he was trying very hard to offer it up to both her and his father. It made her think of the wounded little boy trapped behind the façade of the carefully in-control man. She longed to comfort him.

"Thank you," she finally said on a light whisper as the others settled down at the picnic table to eat their pie.

Mason grabbed her hand in his. "No. Thank *you.* For not giving up on me, or my father."

"What made you change your mind?"

He sighed, looked off to the distant tree line behind his property. "Oh, a lot of things, I guess. Mainly, how you've always been kind to my father when I couldn't bring myself to do so. And then he told me right before you got home today about how he'd defended you last night. It reminded me of Daniel. I guess I got to missing my brother, and I thought about…about my father being here. Maybe God's trying to tell me something."

"God only wants you to open up your heart, Mason. Bitterness destroys all the good we have in life. It blinds us to what really matters."

"Me, bitter?" Then he shot her a lopsided smile.

"This won't be easy. I still have a lot to resolve with my father, but I don't want to waste any more time. And...I want you to be proud of me."

"It's a start," Lily told him, then she kissed him lightly to prove how proud she already was of him.

Mason's eyes shone brightly as he gazed down at her. "We've had lots of new starts today—and so far, I like all of them."

"The best is yet to come," she teased, her eyes twinkling.

Mason pulled her close. "When this week is over and Curtis is safely back at the lake, I'm taking you away from all of this."

"Oh, really?" Her heart took flight like a seagull.

"Really. We're going on that honeymoon, to the condo in Corpus Christi."

"I like that idea."

"Good. It's a date, then?"

"It's a date."

Lily looked up to find Curtis's deep-set eyes on them. And a smile on his craggy face.

Later, when the moon glowed like a guiding beacon in the sky and the stars twinkled like candle flames in the night, Mason stood out on the small, secluded balcony of his bedroom, waiting for Lily to join him.

At the sound of her swishing nightgown, he turned to find her silhouetted against the backdrop of lamplight, her eyes shining bright, her smile hesitant and sweet.

He held out a hand to her and she came to him.

"Mason, is this wrong?"

Hearing the tremble in her voice, he tugged her into the circle of his arms. "Lily, you're my wife. You're wearing my ring. There's nothing to hold us back now."

"I did take a vow," she said, her head cradled against his chest.

"So, are you only doing this to honor a vow, or do you really want to be my wife?"

"I want to honor my vow, *and* I want to be your wife," she said.

"No regrets?"

"No regrets."

With that, they went back inside, shutting the balcony doors behind them, shutting the world out as they discovered, at last, the joy of being married.

Chapter Fourteen

The next week passed in a joyous haze for Lily. She felt closer to Mason than she ever had, and Mason and his father seemed to be reaching a truce of sorts.

During the day, she and Curtis worked on getting the yard in shape, and each night over dinner, Curtis and Mason worked on their fledgling relationship. Although the conversation was polite and stilted at times, Mason had been very patient with his father.

With the help of two neighborhood college students that Reverend O'Neil had recommended, Lily hauled sacks of manure and peat moss, along with various bedding plants and shrubs, in her new blue pickup. A big dump truck delivered another load of dirt, which the boys shoveled and packed to form the beds Lily had pictured in her mind. Curtis mostly supervised from the shade, at Lily's insistence, telling the helpers how to follow her drawn diagrams to the letter. And at his insistence, Lily allowed the strong helpers to do most of the heavy work.

At the end of the week, Mason invited Pam and Robert over for dinner, and to show off Lily's handiwork.

"I still want to build some more trellises and arbors," Lily told Pam as they toured the backyard. "And I'll want to plant some bulbs for next spring, maybe some clematis."

Azaleas nestled underneath the tall pines toward the back of the yard, while a running rose flourished underneath the arbor near the open pool area. Two oak saplings, and other smaller beds made up the finish, complete with Mexican heather, impatiens and lush ferns spilling out from raised beds surrounding the patio.

"Lily, it's so lovely," Pam told her as they walked around the perimeter of the big yard. "You should start your own landscaping business. I'll definitely be your first customer."

"Really?" Lily beamed with gratitude. "I'd love to help you out. Just tell me when."

Pam grinned and nodded toward Robert. "Well, we've set the date for a fall wedding. And we've found the perfect house, not too far from here, but not nearly as big and fancy as this thing." She waved her hands at the house looming in front of them. "Enough room for a couple of kids, though."

Lily's own jolt of disappointment didn't show on

her face. She was truly happy for her friend, even if she would never know the joy of being a mother herself. "That's wonderful. How about we get together in a few weeks and you can show me the house and yard?"

"Great." Pam waved to Mason and Robert as they came around the corner. "Hey, Bob, I've already hired our landscaper." She pointed to Lily.

Robert grinned. "Good—that'll save me a bundle. That firm we talked to the other day charged way too much."

"Careful, buddy," Mason cautioned. "My wife hasn't quoted you her prices yet."

"Good point," Robert countered. "Although I would think I'd get a discount for being your best man."

"Consider it done," Lily told him as they all gathered to go in the back door.

Inside, they found Curtis hard at work making a large salad. Lily had discovered that Mason's father was actually a very good cook, but he had never told her where he'd learned his culinary skills, and she hadn't pressed him for any answers. Like Mason, Curtis didn't like to talk about himself that much.

"That smells good," Mason said, his hand centered on Lily's back.

"It's Curtis's recipe," Lily told him. "Roasted pork tenderloin with herbs and new potatoes."

"I didn't realize you could cook," Mason said as

he watched his father expertly slicing cucumbers into wafer-thin circles.

"Navy," Curtis said on a huff, then turned back to his salad creation.

"I didn't know you were in the navy," Mason replied, then shrugged. He'd tried to avoid the past when talking to his father. In fact, they'd kept everything light, mostly focusing on small talk, like two strangers. Maybe it was time he finally asked his father where he'd been all these years and why he'd left in the first place. Later he'd do just that.

"Time to eat," Lily announced after a few more minutes of small talk. She led Pam and Robert into the formal dining room.

Mason waited for Curtis. "Are you coming?"

"Yeah, got to bring in the salad. Grab that bottle of dressing, will you?"

Mason found the bottle of what looked like freshly made dressing, then stopped in front of his father. "You know, we need to sit down and really talk. I've been meaning to do just that, and you'll be leaving Saturday."

"I'm ready to talk whenever you are, son."

Mason wasn't so sure he was ready, but he had to find the answers to the questions that had colored most of his life. He had to know the truth.

And, in spite of his earlier stubbornness regarding his father, he now agreed with Lily. He had to let go of the past and all the bitterness. Because he loved her and respected her wisdom and her undying faith that all would turn out for the best, he now had the courage to get on with his new life, with the woman he loved.

Dinner started out pleasant. Curtis seemed more relaxed than Mason had ever seen him, and the food was surprisingly delicious.

"My compliments, Mr. Winslow," Robert said as he finished the last bit of bread pudding left in his dish. "Where did you learn to cook like this?"

"Navy," Mason offered before Curtis could respond, his gaze flying to his father's craggy face. "At least that's what he told me earlier."

Curtis nodded, then lowered his head. "Started out in the navy, after…after I left Uncertain."

The silence that followed only made Mason want to shout out all the questions zooming through his mind. "Where did you go?" he finally said, his tone quiet and reserved.

Curtis looked up, directly at Mason. "Son, I've been all over the world. After the navy, I worked as a chef on a cruise line, did some truck driving for a large food company, then finally wound up working as a cook for one of them fancy hotels over in Shreveport."

"Hotels?" Mason shot up in his chair, all patience and civility gone. "You worked over in Shreveport, and didn't even bother to come home?"

"I didn't think I was welcome."

"You were right."

Lily sent him a cautious look. "Mason—"

"I'm sorry, Lily," he replied, thoroughly disgusted with both himself and his father. "I just don't understand."

"I think we need to head on out," Robert said as he stood up. He turned to face Curtis. "We really did enjoy the meal, sir."

Curtis stared at his own half-eaten dessert. "Thank you."

Pam lifted out of her chair, her sympathetic gaze holding Lily's. "Call me.... I'd love to have you help with our landscaping."

"I'll be happy to help," Lily told her. "Here, let me see you to the door."

Mason just sat there, his eyes centered on the man who was supposed to be his father. Giving his friends an absentminded wave goodbye, he twisted in his chair. "Is that why you came home? Did you gamble all your money away?"

"I don't need money," Curtis told him, his chin jutting out in defiance. "I'm not a gambler. I just needed a job, is all."

"And how long did you work in Shreveport?"

"About a year. Started right after they opened up the first boats on the Red River."

Lily came back into the dining room then. Her warning look didn't stop Mason, however. "Do you realize that the whole time you were there, your son lay dying in that lake house? Just a few minutes away, just a short drive over the state line, and you could have seen him."

"I didn't know," Curtis said, his voice shaky. "I didn't know—"

"No, you didn't care," Mason told him, the floodgate of his emotions causing him to shout. "How could you be so close, and not even bother to come back home?"

Curtis looked up at last, his eyes watering, his mouth trembling. "I was afraid, son. Afraid you'd do exactly what you did when I showed up at the wedding—turn me away."

"Yes, and I should have stood by that decision," Mason replied, his eyes dark with pain and rage. "I don't know what I was hoping for here, by letting you into my life again."

"Probably the same thing I was hoping for," Curtis said. "A second chance."

"I don't need a second chance with you," Mason countered. "You never gave me a first chance."

"I didn't leave because I didn't love you, son," Curtis said, tears now falling down his face. "I..."

"You what?" Mason stood, his face red, his expression grim. "Why did you leave, Curtis? Why did you abandon your family?"

Curtis tried to stand, but his wobbly legs gave way. He grabbed the table, causing glassware and plates to shimmy and bang against each other.

Mason caught him before he passed out, then gently settled him back in his chair, his anger changing to concern. "Daddy?"

Lily raced to Curtis. "Curtis, can you hear me?"

"I'll be all right," Curtis said on a weak voice. "Medicine, in my pocket."

Mason reached inside the chest pocket of his father's cotton shirt, then pulled out a small vial of prescribed pills.

"Nitroglycerin," he said, his gaze flying up to Lily's face. Without another word he opened the vial and forced a pill into his father's drooping mouth.

For what seemed like an eternity, Mason watched his father's face. When some of the color returned, he touched a hand to Curtis's arm. "How are you feeling now?"

"Better," Curtis said, the effort taking his breath away.

"Should we call 911?" Lily asked.

Curtis's bony hand shot out to grab her arm. "No, I'll be all right. Just a spell with my ornery heart. It's passing now, though."

"Let's get him to his room," Lily told Mason.

He nodded slowly, then indicated the stairs. "He's too weak to go up. Let's put him in the room down here."

Together they led Curtis to the nearest bedroom and settled him underneath the bedcovers.

"I can stay with him for a while," Lily offered.

"No." Mason sank down in a chair near the bed. "Let me stay."

"Don't upset him again," Lily warned, a hand on Mason's arm.

"I won't." Mason looked up at her then, his heart

filled with a new agony. "He...he's sick, Lily. His heart—"

"Is broken," Lily replied. "And I think he came home to find some sort of healing."

"Or to die," Mason said, his voice barely above a whisper. "And the way I've treated him..."

"You had your reasons, but now we have so much more to be concerned about. You'll be okay, Mason, and hopefully, so will your father." Lily kissed him, then quietly left the room.

Mason sat there in the darkened room, his eyes never leaving his father's face. He listened as Curtis took long measured breaths, then watched and wondered, and relived all the pain and all the bitterness of knowing his own father had left him all alone. And now, suddenly, he could see with such a vivid clarity he had to shut his eyes to the truth, that he had been doing the exact same thing to his father, to pay him back for all those years of misery.

Mason had tried to give Curtis a taste of his own medicine. He'd abandoned his father there at the lake, on the night of his wedding. He'd left without any qualms, while Lily had tried to warn him, had tried to tell him that this wasn't the way to go about things. He'd deliberately pushed his father away at every turn, refusing to listen, refusing to talk about the obstacles between them, refusing to give any slack. But now, right this very minute, as he watched Curtis struggle with each breath, Mason knew in his heart that none of that had brought him any comfort.

Indeed, his acts of self-righteous punishment toward his father had only brought him more misery.

Maybe it *was* time for that second chance between them. Maybe it was time to ask the questions, find the answers, however painful, then get on with forgiving his father once and for all, before it was too late.

As if sensing his son's burning questions, Curtis opened his eyes and spoke into the darkness. "It was your mama, son. She kicked me out."

Mason sat up straight, staring over at the slight figure on the bed. "What do you mean?"

"I always was a heavy drinker, and I loved the nightlife. I stayed out one night too many for your mama's liking, I reckon. She was a churchgoing woman, and she didn't take too kindly to my backsliding ways."

Mason sat there, thinking how simple the truth was, yet how very complicated. A couple of short, terse sentences and he had the explanation he'd so longed to hear. But he didn't like what he was hearing.

"I don't remember you drinking," he said. But he did suddenly remember the fights, the bitter, nightlong fights. Had he purposely blocked them from his mind?

"So, all those times when Mama told us you were working late, you were really just staying out late?"

"That about sums it up. She hid it pretty well when you were little. But when you got bigger, your brother, Daniel, started asking questions. She didn't want y'all to know the truth about your old man.''

"You both hid it pretty well," Mason said now, memories pouring through his system. Maybe he'd denied those memories all this time, because he didn't want to know the truth.

"I wasn't a mean drunk," Curtis told him. "But I did turn into something ugly when I drank. I wanted to have things my way, all the time. I expected your mama to either join up with me, or let me alone to seek my comfort in the bottle."

"Did you ever try to stop?"

"Oh, yeah. We'd fight, then I'd promise to do better. I'd find steady work and your mama would forgive me all over again. But soon I'd start staying out with the boys, partying to the wee hours. I didn't want to stop. Liked it way too much."

"So you left. You just left us there, while you had a lifelong party?"

"I thought I wanted that kind of life, free of responsibilities and worries. Party didn't last too long though. Once I got out there on my own, I found out real quick that kind of life was about as hollow as a rotten log. Didn't take long for me to stop drinking with my buddies and start drinking alone. And let me tell you something, son, that's about as lonely and low as a man can get."

Mason actually felt sympathy for his father. Apparently Curtis had suffered the consequences of his life-style in more ways than one. Mason realized there were all types of loneliness, and his father had certainly experienced pain because of his actions. Maybe that should be punishment enough.

"Did you ever try to come back?" he asked now.

"Plenty, but she always turned me away. Said she didn't want you boys to grow up like me."

Mason's sigh shuddered through his body. "Oh, we grew up all right. Daniel overcompensated by being rigid in his convictions, while I set out to conquer the world on my own terms."

"Better than living with a no-account drunkard."

"Was it really better, Daddy? Was it really for the best?"

"Your mama thought so. And after a while, so did I." He raised himself up off the bed, his eyes centered on Mason. "But I never, ever stopped loving you boys. I wanted…I wanted what was best for you, and at the time that didn't seem to be me."

"So you stayed away."

"I stayed away. Then I got the chance to work in Shreveport, and I hoped…well, never mind what I hoped. I was still a coward, so I stayed away. I heard things here and there, about you—your big company—and about Daniel's business on the lake. But I didn't know he was sick, son."

"He didn't tell many people," Mason admitted. "Too proud."

"A family trait," Curtis said on a quiet whisper. Then he took a breath and said, "I stopped drinking five years ago."

Mason nodded. "Well, that's something anyway."

"Yeah, but I'm half-dead because I waited so long. My heart's shot, and I reckon my liver ain't far behind. I had to retire way too early."

"Did you come home because you're sick?"

"No, I came home because I'm still well enough to make amends. Except I waited too long." His voice trembled again. "Daniel's dead, and you—you'll never find it in your heart to forgive me."

Mason couldn't argue with that, but he did know that tonight his heart had opened and shifted enough that most of his bitterness had sifted out. "I'm trying, Daddy."

They sat silent for a while, then Curtis asked, "Why did you marry your brother's widow?"

Mason didn't want to talk about that, but something told him his father would understand. "Because I love her," he said simply.

"Did you love her when she was married to Daniel?"

"Yes," he admitted. "But I didn't act on that love. I stayed away, and let them live their lives. I could never do anything to disrespect the love they shared." He stopped, thought things over, then added, "But when Daniel died, he must have known. He left a stipulation in his will, based on the laws of the Old Testament. He wanted me to marry Lily."

Mason heard Curtis swallow. Then his father said,

"Your brother was a loving, forgiving man, wasn't he?"

"Yes, he was," Mason said. "He was harsh at times, and hard to understand, and he always held everyone at a distance, but he had a good heart. He was well respected and...Lily loved him in her own way."

"That's good. That's good. And she loves you, too, son. I can see that clear enough," he said as he lay back down.

Mason listened as his father's breathing became steady, then he got up and went over to the bed. Curtis was asleep. Mason reached out a hand to touch his father's own bony hand. Then he closed his moist eyes and whispered a prayer.

"I'm trying here, Lord. I am trying so hard. Help me, please, to understand. Help me to let go of this pain, this emptiness."

He squeezed his father's hand and left the room.

Later, as Mason lay beside his wife and held her close, he marveled at the turn of events in his life. It was as if God had truly answered the prayers to which Mason hadn't even put a voice. He was married to a woman he loved completely, and his father had come home.

Armed with the truth at last, Mason could look back now and see that his mother, Elly, had been just as bitter as he'd turned out. She'd suffered so much, but she'd turned that pain inward and she'd

unintentionally forced it onto her sons, too. She'd
never allowed for any second chances. In her own
way, she'd been as rigid as Daniel and as indifferent
as Mason. Family traits.

Now that he and Curtis had talked things out, Mason felt a new sense of peace. They still had a long
road ahead of them, but he was determined to see
things through with his father. And he knew he
could do that, with Lily by his side.

She turned to face him. "Can't sleep?"

"No. I want to take him to a heart specialist, here
in Dallas. We might have to postpone our trip to the
beach."

"I don't mind," she told him. "I don't need the
ocean."

And he knew she was being honest. Lily didn't
need the things that most people coveted. She only
needed someone to love, and her faith in God to
guide her through life. Mason suddenly needed both
of those things, too.

And for the first time, he also longed for one more
thing to make his life complete. The one thing he'd
vowed he'd never want in his life, because of his
misguided beliefs regarding his own father.

He longed for a child. But he knew that was the
one thing he and Lily could never have. He could
accept that though, if only Lily would grow to love
him in the same way he loved her. There would be
no baby with which to share their love and joy, but

Mason knew they could be happy together. He'd see to it.

"You're going to have a baby," the doctor pronounced to Lily a month later, his smile beaming like a herald's golden trumpet.

"I...me?" she squeaked, her mind racing with disbelief. At Pam's insistence, she'd come in for a routine checkup, a luxury she could never afford before, and even though she'd been feeling a little tired, she'd never dreamed she might be pregnant. "But Dr. Simms, I can't have children."

"Nonsense! What on earth ever gave you that idea?"

Lily clutched the hospital gown, her hands automatically going to her stomach. "We—my first husband and I...tried for ten years."

"Did you ever go to a doctor for advice?"

She thought back over that time, thought about the humiliation, the disappointment, the condemnation in Daniel's eyes. "I tried a couple of times—specialists here and there—but Daniel didn't believe in doctors and we didn't have any insurance to cover all the tests. He didn't want me taking a lot of fertility drugs, either. Then he got sick with cancer, so we just stopped discussing it altogether. He always said we would have a child if God saw fit for us to have one."

"Well, then, *you* can thank God for answering your prayers now," Dr. Simms replied. "Lily, maybe the problem wasn't so much you. Maybe it had something to do with Daniel's illness.''

Lily didn't want to believe that, but it made sense. Since they'd never officially consulted any experts, though, she'd always blamed herself. And maybe she had been right to do so, since Daniel had been a healthy man up until a couple of years ago.

"What's the matter?" the doctor asked, concerned. "Aren't you happy about this baby?"

Lily looked up, her eyes watering. "Oh, you can't know how very happy I am. I didn't think I'd ever be able to have children. Yes, I'm happy."

Assured that she was all right, the doctor left her with instructions to eat healthy, get plenty of rest and take her prenatal vitamins. "And don't forget your monthly checkups."

Lily got dressed, and still in a daze, left the doctor's office. How would she ever tell Mason? How could she accept that this miracle had actually happened to her?

"Oh, Daniel," she said as she drove down the interstate, tears of joy streaming down her face. "Oh, Daniel, I'm so sorry I could never give you this gift."

Then she remembered Daniel's letter and his words to her about giving Mason a child. A rush of guilt eroded the joy coursing through her system. If she had loved Daniel the way she loved Mason, would they have conceived?

Lily pulled into the driveway and stopped the

truck, then sat there to stare at nothing and everything, her gaze missing the brilliant flower beds
she'd planted just weeks ago. "Maybe I was barren,
Lord," she said, her prayer sounding hollow in her
ears. "Maybe I was as barren in spirit as I was physically. Oh, Dear God, I ask You to help me now.
Help me to understand, help me to give this child a
deserving life. And please, Lord, forgive me. Forgive me for not loving Daniel enough to give him
the child he wanted so badly."

"He now has the best doctors money can buy,"
Mason told her a few days later as they sat in the
den, watching the evening news. Curtis was in his
room—his new room downstairs that had officially
become his for as long as he needed it. Somehow,
through an unspoken agreement, and after weeks of
seeking out heart specialists, he was now living with
Mason and Lily.

"That's good," Lily said absently. She was glad
for Mason and his father. Since that night all those
weeks ago when they'd finally opened up to each
other, their relationship had taken on a new meaning.

Mason was calmer now, more centered. And very
solicitous of his father. Lily now knew the whole
story, too, and marveled at how Curtis had accepted
his lot in life, thinking he wasn't worthy of his sons'
love.

Lily didn't want her child to ever have to suffer through what Mason and Daniel had suffered.

Her child.

She touched her stomach, her gaze seeking out her husband. Somehow she had to tell him about the baby. Every time she planned to talk to him about it, something held her back. She told herself Mason was too worried about Curtis right now, that he was too busy with his latest construction project over in Tyler to deal with this bit of news. But she'd put it off too long already, and she was fast running out of excuses for her constant tiredness and occasional morning sickness. Soon, she thought with a fleeting joy, she wouldn't be able to hide her pregnancy any longer.

She watched Mason now. He seemed so content, so domestic sitting there with a cup of coffee and his newspaper. Would he be happy? Would he feel the same joy she felt each time she touched her stomach and thought about the new life inside her? Or would he be upset, not ready to be a father himself when his relationship with his own father was still so tenacious?

Mason listened to the weather report, then started talking about Curtis again. "He's improving every day. We can't cure him, but with the new medicine and a good, proper diet to strengthen him up and clean up his arteries, he should be able to live here comfortably for a very long time."

"That's wonderful." Lily's mind raced in turmoil, caught somewhere between bliss and torment. She'd wait a few more days, then tell Mason. Maybe when they finally took that promised honeymoon trip that they kept having to postpone. Yes, the beach would be the perfect setting to announce that they were going to be parents.

Mason must have sensed her distracted mood. "You don't mind that he's staying here, do you?"

"Of course not," she told him, patting his hand. "Don't even think that. I wanted him here in the first place, remember?"

"You know," Mason said, taking her hand in his as he nodded, "I was so angry at him, but I've talked to Reverend O'Neil about that. He's helped me see that I have to pray about everything, and learn to be patient and forgiving."

Lily nodded. "I'm so glad you consulted him. He's a good counselor." She'd probably go by and see the preacher herself this very week.

Mason ran a hand through his hair, then sighed. "Yeah, because of my anger, because of what Curtis did, or what I believed he did, that's the reason I never wanted children. Can you imagine someone as bitter and messed up as me bringing a child into this world? I didn't want to turn out like my own father. I was afraid I'd abandon my own child, maybe not physically, but...I didn't have it in my heart to risk such a thing."

Lily went still, her heart turning to shards of crystal that shattered with each beat. *Mason didn't want children?* "We never did discuss children, did we?"

Mason turned his head, a frown centering his forehead. "No, and I guess it's a good thing. I'm sorry, though, that you can't have a child, Lily. And I'm sorry now that I never really wanted one, but we have each other, and that's enough for me."

That's enough for me. At one time she would have agreed with him that having each other would have to be enough. But now—

Then a thought pierced Lily's subconscious—a vicious, ugly thought that left her cold with dread and doubt.

"So you don't want children. And I couldn't— can't have children. How convenient. Mason, is that why you agreed to marry me?"

Chapter Fifteen

Mason dropped his newspaper to stare over at his wife. The stunned, hurt expression on Lily's face tore through him like sharp-edged lace. Did he tell her part of the truth, that her not being able to conceive had played a part in his decision to marry her? Or did he tell her the whole truth and confess that he loved her, had always loved her, and he now wished for a child of their own? No, if he told Lily that now, it would only add to her misery, since she could never grant him that wish. But he could convince her that he loved her. Maybe.

But what if she wasn't ready to accept his love? Maybe it would be better to keep things light, more businesslike, even though this marriage had gone way beyond a simple arrangement just for the sake of convenience. Torn and in despair, he could only sit there staring at her.

"It's true, isn't it?" Lily said, obviously taking his silence as a sure confession as she got up to pace around the room. "You said there were practical reasons for this match. And not having children fit right in with your own agenda, didn't it?"

"Lily." He reached out a hand to still her, while he tried to still his own fearful heart. "I'll admit the thought crossed my mind. No, I never wanted children, never needed a family of my own. But it was because—"

"Because you've always had to put business first," she interrupted. "You told me that going in. Told me you had your work and your life and all you needed was someone to organize things and give you a proper home—a proper wife to show off to all your executive friends."

Before he could respond, she whirled away from his touch. "Well, I'm not that kind of woman, Mason. I'm not a trophy or a prize. I'm just plain-Jane Lily, from the wilds of Caddo Lake. I'm just a…a barren, backwoods widow, someone to pity and feel guilty over. You tried to convince yourself you wanted this, tried to believe you were honoring your brother's dying wishes, but deep down inside you were just being Mason—looking ahead to the benefits. And apparently, the benefits of not having to deal with a child far outweighed any shortcomings I might bring into this marriage."

Mason couldn't believe she saw herself or him in

the ways she'd just described. "Lily, that's not how I viewed this. Not at all."

But as he sat there, he had to admit that at first, that's exactly how he'd pictured this marriage. Convenient, with a companion he cared about, with no strings attached and no children to force him to face his own shortcomings. Ah, but all of that had changed so very much.

But how did he tell her that now, when she looked so dejected, so hurt, so broken and vulnerable? If he told her that he loved her, she wouldn't believe him. Not now. Maybe not ever.

So instead he said, "Since you couldn't have children, I didn't think it would matter one way or the other how I felt about not wanting them. I'm sorry."

"So am I," she replied, silent tears coursing down her face. "I—I had such hopes for us, Mason. I actually thought—"

He got up then to pull her into his arms. Somehow he had to make her see the truth. "Lily, remember I told you I'd never do anything to hurt you. That much is true. I told you I'd be here, that you'd always have me."

She pushed at him, forcing him to let her go. "Yes, and now I can see how easy it was for you to make that promise. You figured you'd take care of me, pamper me, parade me around like some sort of glorified business asset, but you never really committed to our vows, Mason. You never stopped to think about the emotional side of marriage. You were just fulfilling some sort of misguided duty to your brother.''

''That's not true—''

But Lily was done with listening. Lifting a hand to stop his explanation, she said, ''We both came into this marriage for all the wrong reasons, and now it's beginning to tell on us. We're paying the consequences of our actions, Mason. We were wrong to get married, and now we can at least be honest about that.''

Mason watched as she left the room, his heart feeling as if someone had just put a vise to it and squeezed it in two. He told himself to go after her, to tell her that he loved her so much, he'd do anything to show her that love. But all he could do was sink down on the couch and put his head in his hands.

And that's how Curtis found him.

''Everything all right, son? I thought I heard shouting in here.''

Mason looked up at his father. Not bothering to hide the tears burning his eyes, he wiped a hand across his face. ''No, everything is not all right. Lily and I had a terrible fight, and I need to be by myself right now.''

''No, you don't,'' Curtis said as he sat down beside his son. ''I think what you need more than anything right now is a father. And I'm here, son. I'm here.''

Mason fought hard to grip the flood of emotions

breaking through the last of his bitterness. But like a crashing wave, all his hurt and anger came pouring out, seeking release. Paralyzed with the fear of losing Lily, he dropped his hands and slumped toward his father.

Curtis caught Mason in his arms and hugged him tightly against his skinny frame. "I'm here, son. At last."

Mason shook as he gripped his father close, the sobs racking his body a gentle, cleansing release. "I love her," he managed to whisper. "But I didn't tell her in time. I waited and now it's too late."

Curtis lifted his son by the shoulders and looked him square in the eyes. "No. It's never too late when you love someone." His own voice shook with emotion. "Look at us, son."

Mason took a long shuddering breath. "You told me you believe Lily loves me. You said you could see it. Why couldn't I?"

Curtis shrugged. "Maybe because you couldn't look beyond your own pain and longing. Maybe because I hurt you so much, you were afraid to see that someone could love you."

Mason nodded, everything crystal clear in his mind now. He wouldn't let her walk away; he wouldn't let her go. He loved her, and unlike his father had done all those years, he wouldn't sit by silently. With a renewed hope, he fell back into his father's strong arms and cried the last of his tears.

* * *

Lily slipped out the back door leading to the garage, a small suitcase in her trembling hand. She was going back to the lake. There she would have her child, there she would ask God to forgive this terrible, terrible mistake she had made in the name of honor.

There was no honor in this marriage. How could there be any honor between a man who didn't know the true meaning of love and a woman who confessed to loving the wrong man?

She'd married Mason because in her heart she wanted to be with him. It was that simple, and that wrong. It didn't matter that Daniel had condoned it, had requested it. She could tell herself that all day long, and it would never matter again. The only thing that really mattered now, was that she was going to have Mason's child. Out of despair, she would find joy.

But she would do it alone.

With that thought, she cranked her truck and slowly backed it out of the open garage, all of her hopes and dreams turning as black and starless as the never-ending night lifting out before her.

Lily arrived at the lake house well after midnight. Tired and exhausted, she went in and went straight to bed. In spite of her broken spirit, it felt good to be back here where she'd always felt safe and secure, and loved. With her bedroom window open to the sounds of late summer, she drifted in and out of a fitful, tormented sleep. But somewhere between her tears and the breaking of dawn, she sent up a prayer for absolution, for redemption, for a second chance to make things right in her life.

"I'm leaving it in Your hands, Lord. I can accept that Mason will never love me, and I can accept that this marriage wasn't meant to be. I only ask that You show me the way, and help me to raise this child with the love and faith that You've always shown me."

About an hour after sunrise, Lily got up to make herself a strong cup of coffee. As she made her way down the hall toward the kitchen, a sharp, severe pain centered in her stomach, causing her to bend over and groan.

"No," she whispered as a cold sweat popped out on her forehead. "Dear God, please no. Don't let me lose this baby."

The pains grew worse. In a panic, she made her way to the phone and dialed her parents' number. Cora answered on the second ring.

"Mama," Lily said, her voice weak. Feeling faint and nauseated, she managed to sink into a chair.

"Lily, sugar, what's wrong? You don't sound—"

"Mama, can you come? I'm at the lake house. I'm sick."

"I'll be right there."

Lily heard the click. Then the ringing of the dial tone merged with the ringing in her ears as she gave in to the swirling blackness and fell in a heap on the kitchen floor.

She was having a beautiful dream where everything was colored in bright, sunny yellows and luminous, crisp whites. Mason was there. He was standing by the lake, a smile on his face. A small child stood beside him, and then another child ran up to greet them. Mason swept the little boy up in his arms and held the hand of the little girl. Oh, what a sweet scene. How precious. They all looked so happy. Lily wanted to go to them, to tell them all how much she loved them, but she couldn't reach them. She couldn't reach them.

She came awake, disoriented and drenched in sweat. Cora stood by her, a concerned look turning her usually serene expression into a frown. "Honey, you were having a bad dream. Are you all right?"

And then Lily remembered where she was and what had happened over the last twenty-four hours. Her parents rushing to her, a siren in the distance, a long trip to the hospital, pain, so much pain. Then sleep, rest, and...hope.

She tried to get up, but Cora pushed her back down. "Oh, no, young lady. Remember what the doctor told us. If you promise to stay in bed, you won't have to go back to the hospital."

Lily sank back against the soft pillows, a sigh of relief coursing through her system. "I didn't lose the baby."

"No, honey, you didn't. And you won't as long as you behave and stay in that bed for the next few days."

Lily touched a hand to her stomach. "The pain's gone and I've stopped spotting. The doctor said it would stop if I just tried to relax."

"And the doctor is right. With all that gardening, you probably tore your placenta a little bit and separated it from the baby. It has to heal up." Cora sat down in a chair she'd pulled up to the bed, a magazine unopened in her hand. "I called Mason."

Lily twisted her head to stare at her mother. "I told you not to do that."

"He has a right to know, Lily."

"And I guess you decided you had a right to tell him."

"No. That's your place. I just told him that you weren't feeling well and that you'd spent the night in the hospital." She tossed her magazine down. "Of course, he's on his way right now. He was full of worry and questions."

Lily hated the tears forming in her eyes. "Mama, I've made such a mess of this marriage. The whole thing was a big mistake."

Cora lifted a brow. "And this baby? Do you believe this was a mistake?"

Lily swallowed back the lump in her throat. "No, this is a…miracle. A gift."

"Was this child conceived in love?"

That was hard to answer, but she couldn't lie to

her mother. "It was, on my part," she said on a soft whisper. Then, as the tears spilled over and ran into a wet pool on the white cotton pillow, she added, "I never told Mason I loved him. I never told him, Mama."

Cora came to sit on the bed, then leaned down to gather Lily in her arms. "He knows, honey. And I think deep in your heart you know that he loves you, too."

"No, he doesn't," Lily sobbed. "This marriage was just another conquest to him, another way to reach a goal."

"Nonsense," Cora chided. "No matter what the two of you believe, you both wanted this, because you both had a deep abiding love for each other."

Lily struggled to stop the tears. "But it's wrong. It's wrong of me to love Mason."

"Did you love Mason when you were still married to his brother?"

Lily thought long and hard about that question. She had often asked it herself. "I loved Daniel and I was faithful to that love in thought and deed. But after he died, after he requested this marriage, it was as if he'd put into action everything I'd tried so long to deny."

"So now you're afraid of loving Mason?"

Lily gripped her mother's hand, hoping to make some sense of her feelings. "I'm afraid, because I love Mason so much more than I ever loved Daniel.

And that's wrong. I should have given Daniel a child."

Cora shook her head. "Honey, you can't go blaming yourself for things beyond your control. You did the best you could with the love you felt for Daniel. But he's gone now, and you're married to Mason. Are you going to turn him away, turn away from a chance at real happiness simply because of your guilt?"

"I don't want to feel this way," Lily admitted. "But I asked God to show me the way, and then—"

"And then you almost lost the baby."

"Yes." Lily couldn't imagine the pain if she did lose this child. How could she ever cope with that kind of grief? How could she accept something so devastating as God's will? His will, or her punishment?

"But you didn't lose the baby," Cora reminded her. "And you won't. You have to be strong, honey, and fight hard to nurture the life growing inside you."

"How do I do that, when I have so many doubts?"

"Watch and pray," Cora reminded her. Then on a practical note, she added, "And you tell your husband the truth."

"I'm not ready for that," Lily replied, turning to bury her face in the pillow.

"Well, you'd better get ready," Cora retorted. "Mason's car just pulled up in the driveway."

* * *

He took the porch steps running, leaving Curtis to amble up the walkway by himself. His father had insisted on coming, but the wild, fast-paced ride couldn't have done Curtis's weak heart any good.

But right now, Mason's only concern was his wife. He'd lived through several nightmares over the last few hours, and now he just wanted to see her face, to touch her hand, to know for himself that she was all right.

Bill Norton met him at the front door. "She's resting, and I'd advise you not to get her all upset."

Mason admired Bill's fierce fatherly love, but at this moment, he didn't care if the man punched him in the face. He wanted to see Lily. "I don't intend to upset her. What's wrong anyway? What happened?"

"We'll let Lily explain," Cora said as she came into the room and held a gently restraining arm on her husband. "She just woke up."

Mason pushed past them to the big bedroom on the other side of the house. When he reached the door, however, he had to stop. Lily lay in the bed, surrounded by puffy cotton and patterned lace, her face turned toward the big, open window that allowed a perfect view of the shimmering waters of Caddo Lake. In spite of her paleness, she'd never looked more beautiful.

"Lily," he called, waiting, his heart bursting with such a protective love, he knew he would have to be honest with her at last, or risk a completely broken heart. He was more than willing to take a risk on love, than losing her forever.

She turned at the sound of his voice, her expression guarded and vulnerable, her eyes dark and luminous with both hope and pain. "Hello, Mason."

He came into the room, then sank down on his knees beside the bed. "Are you all right?"

Silent tears formed in her eyes. "I think I will be. At least, I hope so."

Impatient and worried, he sighed and ran a hand through his tousled hair. "Just tell me what happened."

She smiled softly, then reached a hand to her stomach. "We happened, Mason. Together we caused this."

Misunderstanding, he put his hand over hers there on her stomach. "I'm so sorry, Lily. I didn't mean to make you sick. I didn't mean to make you run away."

"I'm not sick," she said. "Not in a bad way, at least." As the tears streamed down her cheeks, she reached a hand up to his face. "I'm going to have a baby, Mason. Your baby. And yesterday I almost lost it."

Mason felt as if he'd been hit by a tidal wave, his greatest fears colliding squarely with his best hopes. "What?"

"I'm pregnant," Lily replied, sniffling back another flood of tears. "And I know you don't want children, but you won't have to worry. I intend to stay here on the lake and raise our child. I don't want you to feel any obligations.''

Mason stared at her, unsure whether to hold her tight in joy, or shake some sense into her. "No obligations?" he said, the words rising out over the still room. "No obligations toward my own child? How can you even think I wouldn't feel obligated?"

"Our marriage didn't work," she tried to explain. "But something good came of it. It's just that—"

"Just what, Lily? Just that you think I don't feel the same sense of commitment you do? Just that you think I'm not worthy enough to father a child?" At her surprised look, he continued, anger fueling his courage. "Well, let me tell you a few things, Mrs. Winslow. One, I love you. I have always loved you and I will always love you."

He saw the shock in her expression, but kept talking. "That's right. I loved you when I left this lake, but because I respected what you and Daniel had together, I never acted on that love. I stayed away, stayed clear of anything that might be considered inappropriate, but I always thought about you, watched over you, loved you as a friend and a relative."

She tried to speak, but he held a finger to her lips. "And then my brother gave me the one thing I never dreamed I could have—a chance to prove my love to you. So don't ever doubt that love again."

Lily again tried to say something, but he hushed

her. "And two, this baby is mine. Yours and mine, and whether you want to believe it or not, I want a child with you. I didn't want children before, that much is true. But because of you, because of the love and the joy you've brought into my life, I—I want this baby just as much as you, Lily. And that's the complete, honest truth."

Just to prove his point, he lay his head against her stomach and turned to face her, his own tears clogging his throat. "Whether it's wrong or right, I don't know anymore. I only know I don't want to be without you in my life. I love you."

Lily pulled a hand through his hair as a brilliant joy radiated her soul. "I love you, too, Mason."

He brought his head up, face-to-face with hers. "You do?"

"Yes, I do. But I thought my love for you was wrong. I thought God was punishing me by taking away our baby."

"Why would you think such a thing?"

She touched his hair, his jaw, his mouth, with her hand. "Because I love you so much. More than I ever loved Daniel. And I wasn't honest about that love, not with you, and certainly not with myself. I entered into this marriage after finding a letter from Daniel. He said you needed me, but I was afraid to tell you that. I was afraid you didn't really need me at all. So I married you to honor his request—not the one in the formal will, but the personal one he left me in his letter. But I felt so guilty. So guilty."

Her voice cracked and she stopped, a single tear slipping down her cheek.

Suddenly Mason saw everything she'd been fighting against. She loved him as much as he loved her, but she felt such a tremendous guilt because of that love that she had refused to acknowledge it.

"Lily," he said as he pulled her into his arms. "Lily." He kissed away her tears, then told her, "Let's start all over. Let's make a new commitment to our vows, to our love, to our child. Daniel wanted this for us, maybe because he saw what we couldn't see, maybe because he was a kind, loving man who knew what sacrifice was all about. And I have to believe that if we ask God to guide us and forgive everything in the past, He'll allow this for us, too. He wants us to be happy, Lily."

"Does He?" she asked. "Do we deserve any happiness?"

Mason nodded. "If we make a new commitment to our faith, if we let go of all the old hurts and the pain, I believe God will give us this chance, Lily. It worked with my father and me, and now it can work with us."

"I do love you," she told him. Then she kissed him. "I thought I'd lost you."

"I told you," he reminded her as he guided her back down on the pillows. "You still have me, Lily. You will always have me."

As she gazed into his eyes, a gentle breeze lifted the lacy curtains at the window, and somewhere off in the distance, a dove's soft coo echoed God's promise, sounding it right along with Mason's words.

"I will not leave you."

It was a pledge to both of them and to their child. And it was all the proof she ever needed.

Epilogue

Mason dashed through the double doors of the hospital maternity ward, a broad grin on his sweat-drenched face.

"It's a boy," he announced to the cluster of people gathered in the waiting room. After all the sighs and words of praise had died down, he added, "And a girl."

Cora clutched her husband's shirtsleeve, her eyes lifting to heaven. "Are they both all right? And Lily. How's Lily?"

Mason clutched his mother-in-law by the shoulders, not caring how ridiculous he probably looked in his scrubs and protective surgical cap. "They are perfect," he said, grinning all over again. "Absolutely perfect." Then because he was so tired and giddy, he let go of Cora then grabbed Bill Norton. "Do you know how amazing your daughter is?"

"Yep, I believe I do, son," Bill said in a voice choked with pride and emotion.

Mason shook Bill's solid shoulders, causing the older man to glare up at him. "And do you know how much I love your daughter?"

Bill chuckled, then after gently extracting one arm away from Mason's giddy grip, patted him on the shoulder and said, "Yes, son, I believe I do."

"What'd you name 'em?" Jeremy asked, his eyes wide.

Mason searched the area until his gaze settled on his own father. "William Curtis and Cora Danielle," he announced with pride.

Bill swallowed hard and looked at his wife, helpless with humility, while Curtis could only stand there and stare at Mason, his mouth open in awe.

"You named your boy after me?"

"And me—I'm the William part," Bill managed to croak. "And hey, Cora here, too, for the girl, I mean. How about that!"

"Yes," Mason said, touching a hand to his father's arm. "And Danielle is a combination of Daniel and Elly—for my brother and my mother."

Curtis nodded, cleared his throat, then looked up, pride evident in his next words. "Your mama would have sure been proud of that."

Pete poked Mason's ribs. "Well, you ain't gonna call 'em all that, are you?"

"No," Mason said, laughing. "We're going to call them Billy and Danni."

"That'll do," Pete acknowledged, giving Mason a thumbs-up sign. "Only use full names in emergencies or dire circumstances, okay? And let me just say from personal experience, having a twin isn't so very bad." When his brother whacked him on the head, he added, "Well, most of the time anyway."

Mason laughed, then threw up his hands. "I've got to get back to Lily and my babies."

"Go," Cora told him. "Tell them we love them and we'll see them all later."

Mason hurried away, then turned at the doors to give the people he loved one last look. After all these months of waiting for his children to be born, after all this time of getting reacquainted with the woman he loved and sharing the joy of their coming parenthood, he knew now it had been worth every moment. At last he felt as if he really belonged in Lily's family.

When he found his wife cuddled between the two most beautiful newborns he'd ever laid eyes on, his heart overflowed with a love so strong that he wondered how he'd ever been patient enough to wait for this moment. And why he'd waited so long to find such happiness.

Lily looked up, sleepy-eyed, as he came close to the bed. "I was having such a wonderful dream," she told him in a new-mother whisper.

Mason touched a finger to his son's perfect little fist. "Tell me."

"I dreamed I saw you standing down at the water's edge, with Billy and Danni. You were laughing and you looked so happy.''

"That wasn't a dream, honey,'' Mason told her, his grin back full force. "That was a dream *come true.*''

"Yes,'' she said, sleep pulling at her words. "It must have been, because this time I was there with you.''

"Go to sleep, darling,'' Mason told his wife. "And remember, I'll be here when you wake up.''

"I still have you?'' she teased, her smile so beautiful, Mason had to suck in his breath.

"You still have me,'' he told her as he leaned down to kiss her and his children. "Always.''

As a new dawn crested outside the hospital window, Mason sat down to watch his family sleep. He'd never felt such peace, such perfect contentment. His father was in fairly good health, his business was prospering and he and Lily divided their time between the big house in Dallas and the house they both loved on Caddo Lake, with Curtis coming and going between each as often as he wished. And now twins. Two precious little babies, created out of love, destined to be nurtured in faith.

What more could a man possibly ask for?

Mason bowed his head and thanked God for his blessings, and…thanked his brother, Daniel, for giving him the chance to love again.

* * * * *

Dear Reader,

Caddo Lake is one of the most beautiful spots on earth. It's partly in Louisiana, partly in Texas, and it has always been a mystery to me with its swamps and cypress trees and dark waters. I enjoyed writing about this great, ever-changing body of water.

I also enjoyed writing about Lily, who was so like the lake she loved, and Mason—the builder, the realist— who was too progressive to ever look back. Sometimes, looking back can be painful, but in order to move forward, we have to face the past. And sometimes, the most simple requests are the hardest ones to honor.

I hope you enjoy reading the story of Lily and Mason. And I hope that if there is something in your past that needs resolving with God's saving grace, that you'll take the time to stop and set things right before you move on.

Until next time, may the angels watch over you while you sleep.

Lenora Worth